'Oh, Sarah!' Jed excla[...] raggedly. 'We can't go on [...] this.'

Past thinking about what he wanted, nee[...] only knowing that it was what she wan[...] Sarah ran to him and buried herself against [...] chest.

Slowly, really quite slowly, his arms came around her, and with gentle soothing motions he held her against him.

Scooping her up, he carried her to the bed and laid her gently down. Lying beside her, he pulled her back into his arms.

'I haven't known what to do,' she mumbled against him. 'How to talk to you, what to say.' She compulsively ran her hand up and down his chest. 'Let me kiss you.'

She continued to stare at him with worried eyes until he slowly drew his head lower and gently kissed her mouth.

Emma Richmond was born during the war in north Kent when, she says, 'farms were the norm and motorways non-existent. My childhood was one of warmth and adventure. Amiable and disorganised, I'm married with three daughters, all of whom have fled the nest—probably out of exasperation! The dog stayed, reluctantly. I'm an avid reader, a compulsive writer and a besotted new granny. I love life and my world of dreams, and all I need to make things complete is a housekeeper—like, yesterday!'

Recent titles by the same author:

BRIDEGROOM ON LOAN
THE RELUCTANT GROOM
THE BOSS'S BRIDE

MARRIAGE FOR REAL

BY
EMMA RICHMOND

First published in Great Britain 2000
Harlequin Mills & Boon Limited,
Eton House, 18-24 Paradise Road, Richmond, Surrey TW9 1SR

© Emma Richmond 2000

ISBN 0 263 81992 2

Set in Times Roman 11½ on 12½ pt.
01-0006-34300

Printed and bound in Spain
by Litografia Rosés, S.A., Barcelona

CHAPTER ONE

FIGHTING back tears, Sarah watched the tall figure below her limp awkwardly down the steps. John Erskine Dane. Jed. Her husband. There would be a look of determination on his face, a grim fierceness not to give in to the pain in his leg; the weakness. How far would he get today? To the crossroads?

I love him, she thought. I love him so much it hurts—but loving him didn't take away the pain of what had happened, the anguish. She didn't blame him for the way he was behaving, of course she didn't. None of it had been his fault. Tomorrow would be better, she promised herself. Tomorrow. Or the day after. And then everything would be all right.

As he disappeared from view, she stared out over the lake. Loch, she mentally corrected. Rain pitted the pewter surface, dripping forlornly off the naked trees. Be patient, the doctor had said. But it was six weeks now, nearly seven, and still the tears kept coming. No warning, no control, just suddenly tears, and that tight ache in her chest. Perhaps they should have returned to Bavaria to be with their friends, but she had thought it would be so hard to weather the sympathy, the kindness. She knew no one here, and no one knew her, or what had happened. They knew Jed, of course. He'd spent part of his childhood here.

'Will you be wanting anything else, Mrs Dane?'

The soft Scottish burr took her by surprise, and Sarah gave a little start. Refusing to turn, she shook her head. 'No, thank you, Mrs Reeves.'

'I'll be away, then.'

'Yes.'

Sarah heard the door close and then resumed her contemplation of the loch. No monsters in this one. All the monsters were in her head. And if she didn't pull herself together soon…Mrs Reeves probably thought she was a pale, weepy little thing; and felt sorry for Jed for having such a wife. Sarah *wanted* to tell her that she wasn't really like this, but words seemed to have gone the way of her wits.

There would be other babies she tried to tell herself. Next time would be all right—but how could there be a next time when her husband slept in a separate room? How could there be a next time when he couldn't seem to even bring himself to talk to her? Hold her? Kiss her? All the warmth and laughter seemed to belong to another life. And yet, she could remember how she had been. She could see herself so clearly: laughing, happy, confident. Young? Immature? she wondered. Perhaps, but for all her slenderness, her seeming fragility, she had always been so strong. Her light brown hair had curled enticingly round her small face, deep brown eyes always so full of mischief. She had always known what she wanted—and she had wanted Jed. Not in a dark, calculating sort of way. She hadn't set out to woo him, trap him, but from the first moment she had seen him awareness had sprung between them, tension.

With three months left of the year she had taken off after gaining her degree, she had visited all the places she had so long wanted to see. With the funds generously given by her grandmother, she'd visited North America, the Far East, China, Columbia, Australia, and then returned to Europe. With her brown hair lightened almost to fair by the

Antipodean sun; her skin tanned to gold, she'd flown into Bavaria—and found Jed.

'I've won a *what*?'

'Balloon trip.'

'*Balloon* trip?'

'Mmm-hmm.' The young man smiled at her, his blue eyes amused. 'Ready?'

'Ready?' she echoed. 'What, *now*?'

'Certainly now.'

'But I've only just arrived!'

'I know.' Taking her knapsack, he walked towards a blue Land Rover with the picture of a balloon on the side. A bemused Sarah slowly followed, and then burst out laughing. This was crazy!

'Nervous?' he asked as he helped her into the vehicle.

'No,' she denied. 'Bewildered, astonished, flabbergasted… And how on earth do I know you're who you say you are?'

'Because in a moment you will see the field, and the balloon and all the people.' He grinned, put the car in gear and drove off. Five minutes later he pulled into the field.

'You can leave your kit in the car; it's the support vehicle.'

Meaning, she assumed, that it was going to

follow the flight. Still puzzled, still bewildered, she collected her camera, made sure her bumbag with her money and passport was safely strapped round her waist, and climbed down. 'I didn't buy a raffle ticket or anything...' she began hesitantly.

'No,' he agreed, 'but we had a spare place and we thought it would be nice to offer it to someone. We watched you get off the coach and we thought you looked like someone who might enjoy it.'

'I will, but...' With a small grin, a little shake of her head, she followed him towards all the activity round the slowly inflating balloon. It was a lot bigger than she'd expected.

She was introduced to the other passengers, the female navigator and the pilot, all of whom spoke excellent English, which was fortunate, because her German was virtually non-existent. They were given instructions on what to do in the event of this or that, including the position to adopt if there should be a crash-landing, and then, before she was sure she was ready, she was boosted into the basket. They were told to duck down as the burner was fired, which was very hot, she discovered. No wonder the pilot and navigator wore hats—she was sure she could smell singed hair! And then, without drama, just as the sun nestled against a distant peak, they began to rise. Gently, almost imperceptibly, the basket left the ground.

Allowed to stand once more, they all stared down at the rapidly retreating ground. No jerking, no sudden lurch, just a gentle rise that took them ever higher. Shadows lay along the fields and everywhere looked mystical as the slowly setting sun spread its dying light across the beautiful landscape. Well, she had wanted to see Bavaria, and this was certainly a very good way of doing so.

The driver of the support vehicle waved and they all waved back, like children. It was one of the most incredible experiences of her life. She didn't think she had ever known such an utter feeling of peace. Apart from the intermittent flare of the burner, the whoosh of sound, the heat, everything was silent—and then a dog began to bark somewhere below, and she smiled. She didn't want to talk to the others, and perhaps they felt the same, because they were all quiet. A time to think, reflect on the insignificance of human beings.

With very little room to move in the basket that was divided into four sections for the passengers and navigator, and a smaller section for the pilot, they all politely shuffled round so that each could get the best view, take their photographs. The pilot began to explain in both English and German where they were, their speed, pointing out distant towns and villages. But Sarah was barely listening as they floated in a sky that was that beautiful blue that sometimes occurred before darkness descended. Soaring across peaks and valleys, Sarah watched it all and thought she could stay up here for ever, free, unhampered, and tried to impress everything into her mind so that she would always have these feelings.

The hour they were allotted soon passed and as the sun dipped to the distant horizon they were instructed to put their belongings into the pouches provided before they began their descent.

'Do you land just anywhere?' she asked the pilot curiously.

'Sometimes,' he laughed. 'Unable to control the wind, we go where we must. Look for a field where the crops have been lifted or cut. Somewhere smooth without power lines or too many trees. Most of the farmers or landowners know us, and we generally offer

them a free balloon trip in thanks…'
Breaking off, he stared down in concentra-
tion, and then instructed them to assume the
crash positions. He spoke to his navigator,
who was trying to raise someone on her wal-
kie-talkie, and Sarah heard something about
a ten-knot wind before they were suddenly
thrown sideways as they rapidly picked up
speed. Unable to see from her crouched position, eyes wide, she waited for whatever
was going to happen. A small bump, she assumed.

A tree thrashed against the side of the basket and then they hit something, and it wasn't
a small bump at *all*. The edge of the basket
caught the ground first and Sarah stupidly assumed that was it, that they were down and
relaxed her grip, only to be thrown violently
against the man next to her as they rose again
and then hit even harder. With the basket at
an angle, her back pressed against the wicker
side, and her arms braced, they bounced,
hard, five times in quick succession before the
basket finally came to rest—and fell over onto
its side.

Lying on her back, bruised and disoriented,
Sarah watched as everyone scrambled free
and slowly relaxed her death grip on the

safety rope. Someone squatted down beside her and she quickly turned her head. Green eyes examined her with almost hypnotic intensity—and time was suspended.

'Are you hurt?' he finally asked quietly.

'You're English,' she stated stupidly.

'Yes. Are you?'

'Yes.'

'Hurt?'

'No, English. Sorry. Shall I get out now?'

'I think so.'

So solemn, so serious, this stranger with the devastating eyes. He looked cynical and mocking, experienced, older. Competent, as though he'd seen it all, done it all. Perhaps he had. But attractive, and she felt herself tremble. He also looked vaguely familiar.

He helped her to stand, and still she couldn't break her gaze. Never in all her twenty-four years, she thought in bewilderment, had someone had this effect on her.

He nodded with an indifference that hurt, released her, and walked away. He had looked as though he didn't like her. Puzzled, not only by his reaction, but her own, still standing by the basket, she continued to stare after him, and only gradually became aware that everyone, including several unknowns, were helping to squash the air out of the balloon. Leaning into the basket to retrieve her camera, she went to put it down safely, and then changed her mind and quickly snapped a picture of the man who had helped her. Feeling daft, glancing furtively round to make sure no one was looking, she took another one before going to help with the balloon.

'You find him interesting?' a soft voice asked from beside her.

Startled, Sarah turned to the fair-haired young woman standing next to her.

'I am Gita,' she introduced herself shyly, 'from the nearby village.'

Smiling, Sarah shook the proffered hand. 'Sarah Beverley, from England. And, yes,' she finally answered. 'I find him interesting.'

'We also,' she agreed. 'His name is Jed. Our own very important claim to fame. John Erskine Dane. He is now a writer. We like him very much.'

Absently kneading the balloon fabric to get out all the air, Sarah tried the name out on her tongue—and then she remembered. John Dane. 'This is John Dane' from the Middle East, or Africa, or wherever. She'd seen him on the television covering wars, strikes, civil unrest. Crumpled, and sometimes unshaven, he'd stood before a camera and told them what he had seen.

'*Now* he's a writer?' she asked.

'Yes,' Gita responded as both girls continued to watch the tall, dark-haired man who was working at the far end of the balloon. Gita with gentle affection, Sarah with interest.

'He lives here?'

'Yes, for about one year now. He was out walking when he saw the balloon landing and came to help. Perhaps one day we will put up a little plaque,' she teased gently, 'to say that he wrote one of his best-sellers in the calm and peace of our lovely Bavaria.'

'Would he like that?'

'No, I think not. He is a very private man, not one for—extravagance?' she asked doubtfully, unsure of a word that was not in her native tongue. 'He walks in the mountains,' she continued fondly, 'and sits in the café, smiles his quiet smile, and we do not bother him because we think perhaps he is writing in his head and it is best not to interrupt such important thoughts. So we smile and nod and he stays for a little bit more. You will not disturb him?' she asked worriedly.

She would very much like to disturb him,

Sarah thought, but not in the way Gita meant. 'No,' she denied absently. 'I will not disturb him.'

Leaning her forehead against the glass, Sarah wondered, now, if she ever had. Certainly it had never been with the same degree that he had disturbed her. In fact he still disturbed her with his narrow, intelligent face, long-fingered hands that, when he touched her, could play such havoc with her emotions. Dark, thick, silky hair that always seemed to need cutting.

She never had finished touring Europe. She had stayed in the little Bavarian village, not because of Jed, she didn't think—not at first, or not consciously—but she had stayed, and fallen in love. But she had always known, or thought she had known, that she loved him more than he loved her.

And now? Now, she didn't seem to know anything, and soon it would be dark. They would make a pretence at eating, and then she could go to bed. Another day she had got through. What a wretched way to live your life, just getting through it.

She heard the soft snick of the back door closing and panic flared in her eyes. She wasn't ready to face him, not yet, not now. She would go for a walk, she suddenly decided. Without waiting to deliberate the matter, she turned abruptly away, snatched her raincoat off the hallstand and hurried out the front door. Descending the steep steps, she turned in the direction Jed had taken. The soft drizzle soaked her hair in seconds, darkened her raincoat as she walked blindly down to the shore. Waves lapped agitatedly at the pebbles, little slaps of sound that beat counterpoint to her pulse. She tired so quickly now. Not enough exercise, not enough air in her lungs. Feeling dizzy, she halted, looked around for somewhere to rest, and seated herself on a large rock.

With her mind empty, her eyes unfocused, she stared blindly at the loch. You're being so silly, Sarah. All you have to do is talk to him, explain how you feel. Ask him how he feels… And that was the problem, wasn't it? She was afraid to ask him how he felt; what he was thinking, because she had the awful, mind-numbing suspicion that he no longer loved her.

An RAF jet tore through the air above her from the nearby base and nearly frightened her to death. She didn't think she would ever get used to that thunder of sound that seemed to rip the air apart. Hand to her racing heart, she vaguely heard the crunch of pebbles as someone ran along the shoreline, the laboured breathing, but it wasn't until a satchel thudded onto the ground beside her that she bothered to turn her head. A young boy, maybe twelve or thirteen, was staring at her, all eyes and red face from his exertions. He didn't say anything, and neither did she. They examined each other in silence for a few moments, and then he hunched down onto his school-bag and wrapped his arms round his knees.

'They'll go in a minute,' he said with almost humorous resignation.

Who? Who would go in a minute? Glancing beyond him, she saw two young girls, just hovering, but she didn't want to get involved in this, didn't want the distraction.

Breath still labouring, he muttered. 'They are driving me *insane*!'

'Who are they?' She hadn't meant to ask.

'From school.' He shrugged. 'They want to know where I live.' Picking up a handful of pebbles, he began throwing them towards the water. 'And you can imagine what will happen *then*, can't you? It's bad enough now.'

He gave a gloomy sigh. 'Are you the lady who lives with Jed?'

'Yes. You know him?'

He shook his head, glanced furtively sideways to see if the girls were still there. 'What time is it?'

'I don't know,' she confessed. 'Just after half-past three, I think.'

'Will his leg get better?'

'Jed's? Yes.'

'Mum said he was in a car crash.'

'Yes,' she agreed quietly.

'Is that why you're sad? Mum said...' Embarrassed, he broke off.

'Mum said?' she prompted.

'That you cried a lot. Are you from London?'

'No, Bavaria... Well,' she qualified and wondered why on earth she was bothering, 'from Surrey really, but I've been living in Bavaria.'

'Where's that?' he asked without much interest.

'Germany. I think they're going.'

'What? Oh, great.' Scrambling to his feet, he hoisted his school-bag onto his shoulder. 'See you.'

Yes, she thought almost blankly, see you,

but it had been a start, hadn't it? Talking to someone. With a gentle sigh, she got to her feet.

How had his mother known she cried a lot? Sarah wondered as she retraced her steps. Because Mrs Reeves had told her? Her, and everyone else in the small community? As she reached the road she saw that the street lamps had been lit, and now sparkled on the rain drifting silently across their yellow beams. The boy had gone, home to his own fireside, his mother. Had *she* ever followed a boy home from school? She couldn't remember doing so; it had always been the other way around. Until Jed. Jed she would have followed to the ends of the earth. Still would. If he wanted her.

Grasping the rail, she hauled herself up the steep steps than ran parallel to the house. Opening the front door, she found Jed waiting for her.

'You're wet,' he said quietly as she entered. 'Are you all right?'

'Yes. I met a boy—two girls were following him home from school.'

He gave a small smile. 'Yes,' he agreed, 'girls can be the very devil.' Helping her off with her raincoat, he hung it on the rack.

Was she the very devil? she wondered as she followed him towards the kitchen. Perhaps that was what he had thought when she'd plagued him in Bavaria—no, not plagued, she hadn't done that, but she hadn't tried to hide the tension he'd generated in her.

She slowly sat at the kitchen table and watched her husband. His face was sad, his green eyes dull in this light. And the mouth that used to quirk in humour was straight now, uncommunicative. 'Did it used to happen to you?' she asked quietly. 'Girls following you home from school?'

'Sometimes. A long time ago. Are you really all right?'

'Yes,' she agreed and quickly changed the subject. 'How far did you get? To the crossroads?'

'Yes.'

She knew better than to ask how his leg was, if it was painful.

'Shall we eat?'

She nodded, sat quietly and waited for him to dish up the meal that Mrs Reeves had left. She saw that he was trying very hard not to limp.

The accident should have brought them closer together, she thought sadly. The injury

to his leg, the loss of their baby, she con-
cluded in a little mental rush, should have
strengthened their love, but it hadn't. He'd
closed himself off, whether from guilt, or anguish—or a realisation that he no longer
loved her. Was that the reason? And she
didn't know, now, whether she had closed
herself off because he had, or because she just
couldn't cope with thinking about it. He was
such a strong man, so determined, so—self-
willed. She wished she could be like that.
Wished she could be like she used to be.

He looked after her, carefully tried to an-
ticipate her needs, was kind and thoughtful,
but not loving. Not once since the accident
had he kissed her on the mouth. He kissed
her forehead, her cheek, even her hand, but
not her mouth. He trod around her as though
she were made of glass, but he didn't talk to
her; didn't—communicate. Only on a super-
ficial level. But then, she didn't communicate
with him, did she?

Staring down at the stew and vegetables he
placed in front of her, she felt the familiar
lump form in her throat that always preceded
a meal. It made it difficult to swallow. 'Jed…'
she began with some half-formed idea that
maybe now they would talk, but he quickly

interrupted her, as though afraid of what she might say.

'We've been invited to a party,' he said quietly.

She looked up in panic.

'I had a letter this morning. It's a week on Friday. I'll say we can't go.'

'Yes,' she agreed.

'But I suspect they won't give up. It's Fiona and Duncan's fifth wedding anniversary. Old friends of mine. Eat your meal.'

And she tried, she did try, but after two small mouthfuls she lay down her fork. Feeling miserable and desperate, she got quickly to her feet. 'I think I'll go to bed.' Without looking at him or waiting for any comment, she hurried out and up to her room. Closing her door, she leaned back against it, felt the hot flood of tears to her eyes. They couldn't go on like this. Five o'clock was no time to go to bed, but it seemed easier to lie alone in her room than sit with him downstairs not talking.

Feeling weak and shaky, she moved across to the old-fashioned dressing table and sank down onto the stool. Propping her elbows on the surface, her chin in her hands, she stared at herself in the mirror. Her hair, that had

once been so pretty, hung limp and dull round
her small face. Her eyes looked too big, too
dark, with bruised shadows beneath them.
She looked gaunt and ill. And it couldn't go
on. Other women had lost babies...but it
wasn't only the baby, was it? It was Jed.

CHAPTER TWO

MOVING her eyes, Sarah stared at the framed photograph of herself and Jed on their wedding day. The camera had caught them staring at each other as though both were surprised at where fate had brought them.

It had been such a magical summer, the summer of the balloon. Walking into the village with all the others from the trip, she had felt immediately at home. Flower-decked balconies, pretty buildings that had looked medieval, and kindness and warmth from the people. The small inn where they had gone for coffee to wait for the support vehicle had been warm and friendly, and she'd impulsively decided to stay. They'd had a small room in the eaves she'd been able to rent very cheaply, and she'd been able to tour Bavaria from a very nice base.

Jed had been staying there, too. At first, he'd been distant, contained, merely giving a small nod when he'd seen her, which, despite the tension he'd generated, had thoroughly irritated her. For days it had gone on like that, until she'd nearly killed him.

She'd been dashing down the stairs in her usual impulsive fashion, and because the stairs had dog-legged, meaning you hadn't been able to see who'd been coming up if you'd been coming down, there'd been no intimation of danger, only a violent collision on the first landing. Such had been her speed that, even though she'd been lighter than him her momentum had taken them both to the waist-high railing and only his swift action had prevented them both going over into the foyer below. Holding her tight, he'd dropped to the landing and it had been their shoulders that had hit the railing instead of their hips.

Shaking with shock, she'd just stared at him. 'Sorry,' she finally apologised breathlessly. 'Are you all right?'

'Perfectly,' he drawled. Getting to his feet, he walked away and she watched him run lightly up the stairs she'd just descended.

Sitting where he'd left her, she continued to stare after him long after he'd gone. 'Perfectly,' she echoed to herself. She didn't think she was all right; she could have killed them both. She could still almost feel the imprint of his hands on her arms, the tension he generated in her, and despite his relaxed manner, his slow drawl, he'd been as tense as she was, hadn't he?

Still shaking, searching round her for her sketch-pad and charcoal she'd been carrying, she got slowly to her feet and retrieved them. Rather shakily descending the stairs, she went out to her usual seat, and really just for something to do, to take her mind off what had happened, she began sketching a small boy who was playing with a toy car beneath one of the tables. Not that her mind was on what she was doing. It was still on Jed.

The child's father saw what she was doing, and came over to look.

'How much?' he asked in English.

'Sorry?'

'How much do you want for it?'

'As much as you think it worth,' a deep voice said from behind them.

Swinging round, she stared up at the man she'd just almost injured. 'No,' she denied in horror. Shaking her head, smiling at the man, she handed the picture over. 'Please, you're very welcome to it.'

Looking absolutely delighted, he thanked her and went back to his own table.

'Not very businesslike,' Jed disparaged mockingly.

'I don't care. I can't *charge* people!'

'Why?' he asked. 'If people want something, let them pay. You're very good.'

'Thank you, but I still can't charge. Anyway, it's probably illegal. Trading without a licence, or something.'

With a little shrug, he walked off.

Puzzled by his behaviour, wondering why he had spoken when he didn't normally, and feeling even more shaken by an encounter with a man who was seriously beginning to disturb her, she stared rather blankly down at her pad.

'You will do one of my wife?' a soft voice asked.

Snapping her head up in surprise, she stared at the young man before her. 'Sorry?'

'Will you please sketch my wife? At that table over there.' He pointed.

'Oh, yes, of course.' A bit bemused, she did as she was asked, and then another for someone else, and then another.

Frau Keller, who owned the inn, and nobody's fool, took Sarah to one side when she'd finished sketching and offered a proposition.

'You draw, for one hour or two, a day, and I will pay you. More people come, I make more money. It's good for business.'

'Oh,' Sarah said inadequately.

Frau Keller grinned. 'Yes?'

'Am I allowed to take money?' she asked dubiously. 'Don't I have to have a permit or something?'

Frau Keller made a disgusted noise in the back of her throat. 'You stay here rent-free, then. Meals included. Now you be happy?'

Relieved, Sarah smiled. 'Yes. Thank you.' If she didn't actually take *money*, it was probably all right.

'Good, all is settled. Go draw. More people are waiting.'

And so she did. She also wondered if Jed had been behind the offer, and then dismissed the thought. Why would he bother? He didn't even seem to like her. And she strongly doubted he spent any time thinking about her the way she continually thought about him. Every moment not taken up with something else, he was in her thoughts. Irritated and alarmed, she wanted to touch him, discover what it would be like to press her mouth to his, and she kept thinking she ought to go away, leave, before she made a fool of her-

self. Maybe she would have done if he hadn't
come to her room that day. That very hot day.

She'd been out with a party of tourists who
had been staying at the hotel. Returning to the
inn, hot, sticky, she'd run up to her room in
the eaves, longing only for a shower and a
cold drink. She'd opened all the windows, left
the door open to create a draft, and gone into
the minuscule bathroom, the door of which
was beside the main door. She emerged naked
a few minutes later just as Jed walked in.
They met; in fact they collided, and he automatically put out his hands to save her, or
himself.

Time slowed, almost to a stop, as they
stared at each other, and then he kissed her.
No obvious forethought, no plan, he just
kissed her. With hunger, as though he had
been wanting to do so for a very long time.

The initial contact had jerked her into stiff-
ness, but as his mouth continued to touch
hers, gentle and persuasive, she shuddered
and flung her arms round his neck and kissed
him back as though her very life depended on
it. She didn't know how long they kissed; it
seemed like an eternity. She was aware of his
hands on her naked back, aware that he held
something, and then a stray gust of wind blew

the door shut, and they both jumped, jerked apart.

He stared at her for what seemed a very long time, and then he apologised. 'I'm sorry. I shouldn't have done that.'

'Why?' she asked thickly.

He didn't answer, merely gave a rather wry smile. 'There was a letter for you…' he began as he removed one hand from her back. 'Frau Keller asked if I would deliver it.' His eyes held hers, steady, unemotional, waiting, or so it seemed.

She stared at the white envelope he held in blank confusion, then stared back at him, at his naked chest beneath his unbuttoned shirt, and could think of nothing else. Want nothing else. Ignoring the letter, she touched her mouth to his collar-bone, the base of his throat, and the breath he took was deep, ragged. Her damp breasts were against his flesh, her bare thighs against the edge of his shorts, and she wanted him naked, as she was.

'No,' he said softly as he put her away. Pressing the letter into her hands, he turned, opened the door, and walked out.

Shaking, she stared at the closed door. She'd just propositioned him, hadn't she? And been turned down. Embarrassed, mortified, she slumped down on the side of the bed. But he'd kissed her first, hadn't he? Why? Because she was there? Naked? Available? She'd never thrown herself at a man in her life. Staring down at the letter she held in her hands, she shuddered.

He hadn't looked at her body, that was something. He'd kept his eyes on her face. Did that make it better? She had no idea. His wry smile had been a bit shaken, his muscles tense. But not as tense as hers. His girlfriends were probably sophisticated, elegant—experienced. They would have laughed at his kiss, said something witty. And what had she done? Nothing. And now he'd gone.

How would she face him next time they met? Bravely? As though nothing had happened? Avoid him? Yes, that would be best. Except she didn't need to. Over the next two days he was never anywhere in sight. His door remained closed, his table outside, empty. Perhaps he was avoiding her. And she couldn't stop thinking about him, looking for him, going over and over in her mind the way he had kissed her. She could still feel it. Taste it. She'd been kissed a great many times in her life, but no one had ever made her feel like that. So special. So abandoned when he'd left.

And then, on the third day, she saw that his door was open. With no real knowledge of what she was going to do, say, she walked slowly along the landing towards it. She stood outside it for ages, just waiting, breathing slowly, and then she tapped softly. No answer. Pushing the door gently wider, she peeked inside. His room was slightly larger than her own, his bed wider, and there was room for a small table beneath the window. There was a computer, a stack of papers, and, hesitating only momentarily, she walked quietly inside.

'Jed?' she called softly.

Nothing.

There were no sounds from the bathroom, just noises from outside filtering up through the open window. She didn't really remember walking to the desk, or even picking up the top sheet from the stack of papers. She really didn't think she had been *going* to read it; it was just that the words seemed to leap out at her.

There has been talk of a bridge, but in this summer of 1827, if one wants to cross the river to Oberammergau, then one must brave the 250-foot gorge on a raft pulled by oxen. Courage, after all, I tell myself, is only the fear of looking foolish.

'You wanted something?' Jed asked quietly from behind her.

With a little cry of alarm, she dropped the paper as though it were hot, and then bent to quickly retrieve it and put it back on the desk. Warily turning to face him, she began inarticulately, 'I... You weren't here...'

'No,' he agreed unhelpfully as he stood in the doorway, holding a cup of coffee in one hand.

'Your door was open... I'm sorry. I didn't mean to pry. I'd better go.'

He stepped to one side and she began edging towards the door. Halting on the threshold, her back to him, she blurted, 'I can't stop thinking about you.' When he didn't answer, she turned slowly to face him. 'I keep thinking that maybe the kiss wasn't so special, maybe it was just my imagination, maybe it didn't make me feel as I thought I felt... Sorry,' she apologised with a shaky smile. 'I must sound like a teenager. I'm not usually so... I mean, I don't...'

'Don't you?' he asked softly.

'No. Why did you kiss me, Jed?'

'Because I couldn't help myself?'

Eyes wide, she just stared at him.

'You're a very attractive young woman.'

'Am I?' she asked stupidly.

His mouth quirked. 'Yes. Go away, Sarah, I'm too old for you.'

'No.'

'Yes. I sometimes think I was born old. I'm too cynical, too selfish and I'll probably end up hurting you.'

'You don't know that…'

'Yes, I do.'

Still staring at him, wanting him, wishing she had more experience in these matters, she murmured, 'You didn't like me when we first met, did you? Your immediate reaction was…'

'Worry,' he said with soft amusement.

'Worry?'

'Mmm. You stared at me with those big brown eyes, and I knew you were going to be trouble.'

'You were attracted?'

'Yes.'

'Then…'

'No.'

'Then you obviously don't feel as I feel,' she said almost crossly.

He smiled. 'Oh, I expect I do.'

'But you're very strong-willed?' she asked waspishly.

'Very.'

'I'm not asking you to *marry* me!'

'What are you asking?'

Hesitating only momentarily, she murmured, 'To get to know you better.'

Placing his by now probably cold cup of coffee on the desk, he asked quietly, 'How old are you, Sarah?'

'Twenty-four, nearly twenty-five.'

'You look younger.'

'Well, I'm not! And if you're attracted to someone, well, I mean, it's a natural progression to…'

'Kiss?'

'Yes.'

'You know what will happen if we do?'

'I hope so,' she admitted barely audibly. 'Please?'

'You'd better close the door,' he instructed softly.

Breath hitching in her throat, her eyes held by his, she reached shakily out and closed it. 'Now what?'

'Now you come here.'

Staring at him, clear distress in her eyes, she managed, 'To make me feel cheap?'

'No,' he denied gently. 'To try and make you realise what a fool you're being.'

Staring down at her linked hands, she whispered, 'You don't really want me, do you? I'd better go.' Turning, she grasped the door handle, and then hesitated. 'I think I came to tell you I was leaving,' she mumbled. 'There's a bus on Saturday.' Opening the door, she halted again and turned to give him a rather shaky smile. 'It is allowed to make a fool of yourself once in a while, isn't it? It's part of growing up. Goodbye, Jed.'

Hurrying out, she ran along to her own room and closed the door. Heart beating overfast, feeling stupid and young, she collapsed onto the side of the bed, and then stiffened and looked warily up as the door opened and Jed walked in.

'I shall probably regret this,' he said softly. 'I just pray that you don't.' Closing the door, he walked across to her, sat beside her, tilted her chin up with one finger, and kissed her. A soft, gentle, mesmerising kiss. A kiss she was entirely incapable of resisting.

When he lifted his head, she just stared at him. 'Do you want me? Really?'

For answer, he lay her back across the bed and began to kiss her properly, with experience and expertise, and hunger.

Touching his face, his neck, his back with compulsive little movements, she shook with need and a slight fear. When he finally raised his head, she whispered, 'I don't normally behave like this, but you make me feel—things,' she added vaguely. 'I couldn't get you out of my mind. Couldn't forget the way you touched me.'

'And you think I can? I've been resisting you since you landed at my feet. I should be resisting you now…'

'Then why aren't you?'

'Because, like you said, perhaps it is allowed to be a fool once in a while.'

'And making love to me would be foolish?'

Tracing one finger round her gentle face, moving aside the wisps of hair that had escaped from her topknot, he said quietly, 'I don't want to hurt you…'

Putting her hand over his mouth, she said, 'You don't know that you'll hurt me.'

'No,' he agreed.

'Are you afraid that I'll be like that woman in *Fatal Attraction*?'

He gave a quirked smile. 'No.'

'I won't hassle you...'

'You already hassle me.'

'You don't behave as though I do.'

'No,' he agreed, but didn't explain why.

'I'm not very sophisticated.'

'No,' he agreed gently.

'Or experienced.'

Staring down into her big brown eyes, he gave a helpless sigh. He said something that she didn't catch, and then he kissed her again. So gently, so thoroughly, so mind-bendingly sweet that she felt tears prick her eyes.

Not wanting to talk any more, with her heart beating overfast and her hands shaking, she pushed his shirt off his shoulders and he began to undress her, slowly, methodically, eyes holding hers.

Feeling light-headed and wanton, barely able to breathe, she gave in to bliss.

He was so gentle, his hands so sure and experienced, and there was comfort in the fact that he was shaking too. And so began a time of magic. For her, at any rate; she had never been entirely sure about Jed. He wasn't one given to laughter, or extravagance. He was

more wry smiles and quiet amusement. She
didn't know what he thought of her behaviour; he never said. Neither did he ever say
he loved her. Not then. But they were happy,
and, although he never said the words she
wanted increasingly to hear, he was never a
reluctant lover. Quite the opposite, in fact.

Rarely looking to the future, always living
for the day, she teased him, laughed at him,
and made love to him with an energy he said
he found astonishing.

She would leave him alone during the day
whilst he worked. She would visit the friends
she had made in the village, go touring by
bus or bicycle. Sometimes he would go with
her, show her places he had been, and in the
evenings, in the warm velvet darkness of the
night, they would be together, their lovemak-
ing sometimes urgent, sometimes languorous.
How long it would have gone on for if she
hadn't become pregnant, she had no way of
knowing. Perhaps they would have married
anyway, or perhaps they would have parted
and it would have been just a wonderful
memory of a magical summer.

Looking back, she knew the probable date
she conceived. August twenty-fourth. They
had both taken part in the yearly organised

walk in King Ludwig's footsteps, and at dusk, when the bonfires had been lit, when the world had turned red with the reflected glow off the mountain peaks, he had led her back to the inn for the party that had followed.

Eventually, they'd gone up to his room, to his big bed. Maybe they'd drunk too much wine, maybe the warmth of his mouth against hers, the heat of his slender body, had over-ridden the precautions they'd been taking. She had known him four months, and she'd loved him. Hadn't been able to imagine a time when she would not be with him.

She'd hesitated a long time before telling him about the baby, and she truly hadn't wanted to pressurise him, make him feel that he'd had to marry her, and yet, thinking about it now, perhaps she had forced him into mar-riage. Perhaps subconsciously she had known that his honour, his sense of responsibility, would have made him insist.

And perhaps it would have been all right if her pregnancy hadn't been so awful, if she hadn't felt so ill. Sick all the time, irrational, *spotty*. Hormones, the doctor had said sym-pathetically, but even knowing what it had been hadn't stopped her being horrendous, had it? Shouting at Jed, blaming him, bursting into tears all the time... She still *was* crying all the time. And then contrite, begging his forgiveness. And he'd been so kind, gentle— long-suffering? She'd expected him to know what she'd been feeling without being told. Expected him to dance attendance, and yet, never by look, or deed, had he ever intimated that he *regretted* marrying her. Maybe if her parents had been alive, things would have been different. But there had been only Gran and it hadn't seemed fair to drag her out to Bavaria just because her granddaughter had been having a baby. People had babies all the time. Childish, she told herself. You were childish. Spoilt. A spoilt little girl. And underlying it all, there had been guilt. Guilt that somehow it had been all her fault. Guilt for what she'd been doing to him, changing his life when he probably hadn't wanted it changed. And she'd felt resentful, she admitted, that everything had been spoilt. Her happy-go-lucky, carefree existence, all gone.

She'd had a lot of growing up to do, hadn't she?

And then had come the fateful trip to Scotland. She had insisted on going with him. He'd begged her to stay in Bavaria with their friends whilst he did his research for the next book; insisted that he wouldn't be gone long, but no, she'd had to go with him. Poor man. Couldn't even get away for a few weeks of peace and quiet. She'd insisted on doing the driving that day so that he could make notes... Another row—no, not a row. She'd shouted, and he'd gone all quiet. She hadn't been going fast because the road had been winding and hilly. There had been a steep ravine on one side, mountainous outcrops on the other. Then the child had run out onto the road on a bend; a child from a family that had parked to admire the view, and had allowed their three-year-old daughter to get out and stretch her legs. There had been nowhere for Sarah to drive but off the road...

If the safety barrier hadn't already been weak from a previous accident; if the road hadn't been wet... It had all happened so fast with no time to think, plan. They'd crashed through the barrier, sailed out into nothing, and hit a tree. The passenger side had borne the brunt of it, and Jed had sustained severe muscle and nerve damage to his left leg, a gashed forehead, concussion—and she'd lost the baby, which had meant that the reason for their marriage no longer existed. And that was what frightened her so. Only she hadn't been able to tell the doctor that, had she? When he'd gone on about there being other babies, explained about hormone imbalances, about shock and grief…

The soft tap at the door made her start, and she swung round almost guiltily as the door opened, her eyes swimming with tears.

'Oh, Sarah!' Jed exclaimed raggedly. 'You can't go on like this.'

CHAPTER THREE

PAST thinking about whether this was what Jed wanted, needed, only knowing that it was what she wanted, Sarah ran to him, and buried herself against his chest. Clutching him tight, her head against his shoulder, her eyes closed and body shaking, she held him and cried.

Slowly, really quite slowly, his arms came round her, and with gentle soothing motions he held her against him.

'I'm all right,' she blurted tearfully. 'I'm all right, but I can't seem to break out, can't seem to…'

'Shh, it's all right.'

'Is it?' she pleaded.

'Yes.'

But it wasn't. Wrenching her head up, her face tear-strained and puffy, she stared into his eyes. Eyes that looked sombre, hurt, empty.

With one large palm, he gently placed her head back on his chest. 'It's all right, Sarah,' he repeated. 'It will be all right, I promise, but you have to eat. There's nothing of you.'

'I know, and I will. Truly I will.'

He closed his eyes, rested his chin on her hair and felt despair. 'I think you should go back and see the doctor,' he said quietly.

'No,' she denied. 'I'll eat, and go for walks, and then I'll get better.' Lifting her head again, she stared at him, examined his expression, and then raised her palms to put them each side of his face. Staring into his eyes, searching for reassurance, she whispered, 'Don't go just yet.'

His hesitation was momentary, and then he nodded. Scooping her up, he carried her to the bed and laid her gently down. Lying beside her, he pulled her back into his arms, nestled her head into his shoulder and began to softly stroke her hair.

'I haven't known what to do,' she mumbled against him. 'How to talk to you, what to say.' Wanting, needing the feel of him, the closeness, she compulsively ran her hand up and down his chest. He'd lost weight too, and she knew he hadn't been able to write; that he sat in his study doing nothing. 'It isn't your fault, Jed.'

He didn't answer, and she leaned up so that

she could see his face, and then all she
wanted to do was kiss him, have him kiss her.
He had such a beautiful mouth, and she
wanted the loving back, the closeness, but because she didn't know if that was what he
wanted she felt constrained. She'd already
hurt him enough, she couldn't bear to make
things even harder for him. 'Let me kiss you,'
she pleaded and he closed his eyes tight,
looking grief-stricken.

'Don't beg, Sarah,' he whispered. 'Dear
God, don't beg.'

Frightened, unsure, she continued to stare
at him with worried eyes until he slowly drew
his head lower and gently kissed her mouth.

She wanted to savour it, wanted to prolong
it, and so she clutched him tighter, wanted to
feel pain, feel something, *anything*, anything
to dispel the awful numbness that had ridden
her for the past weeks. And when he wanted
to stop, or when she thought he might be going to, she refused to let him, clutched him
tighter and kissed him with fierce delibera-
tion.

'Sarah…'

'No! Make love to me. Please, please,
make love to me!' she cried in anguish. 'I
need to *feel*! Make me feel, Jed,' she pleaded.

'Make me feel.' Her hands feverish, she began to remove his clothes, drag them off any old how, remove her own, and when they were naked, when she could see him, touch him, hold him, she began to kiss him again, force her leg between his thighs. He groaned and rolled her onto her back. Staring down into her pale face, her eyes, his face contorted for a moment—and then he dragged in a deep breath, and gently restrained her.

'You're not ready for this, Sarah,' he managed to force out quietly. 'It's too soon after…' Taking a deep breath, he added, 'Give it a few more weeks. That's not too long.'

Yes, it was, she thought miserably. And she was ready. She was.

'Come on, try and get some sleep.' Settling her back into the duvet, he pulled it to cover them both and closed his eyes.

Even though his arms were round her, his breath was tickling her cheek, she felt lost and alone because it seemed as though he didn't *want* to make love to her. That *he* wasn't ready. But would he ever be? In another few weeks? Or would there then be more excuses?

Eyes wide and fixed on the ceiling, anxious

and without confidence, she whispered, 'Talk to me, Jed. Tell me how you feel.'

'Tired,' he answered slowly, 'and aching. Guilty.'

'You have nothing to feel guilty for. I was the one who crashed...'

'But I should have been driving. It was for my work that we were driving in the first place...'

'It might still have happened,' she whispered.

'Yes.'

'I couldn't go right because of the rocks, the parked car...'

'I know.'

'And if I'd hit the child... Oh, Jed, I go over and over it in my mind. If I'd done this, that. And your leg *will* get better...'

'It isn't my leg!' he denied almost angrily. 'Dear God, I'd rather have lost it than...'

'Don't,' she protested quickly. 'Don't say that. I know it's all my fault...'

'No,' he denied. Thrusting himself away, he rolled to his feet and limped to stand at the window. 'None of it is your fault. None of it! But I don't know how to help you, Sarah.'

Watching him, aching for them both, she

stared at his ruffled dark hair. At his straight back, the taut buttocks that she loved to touch, the angry scars on his left leg. There was a barrier between them that she didn't know how to breach. But she mustn't pressurise him, she thought. Mustn't nag. 'Come back to bed,' she urged softly and hoped it didn't sound too much like a plea.

Turning his head, he stared at her. She looked so fragile, so frail, and he had no more idea than she did how to make things right. Nothing in his life had ever prepared him for this. An intense man, insular, he envied men who seemed to understand women so well. He didn't even understand himself half the time. He could write about passion, feelings, could make things come right in his novels, but real people? Real people defeated him. People were so complicated. So different. His characters could do anything he wanted them to do. Writers shouldn't get married, he sometimes thought.

He wasn't a shy man. He was erudite and confident, articulate, and yet Sarah sometimes defeated him. He felt responsible and guilty and he thought she would probably be a great deal better off without him. A writer's life, of necessity, was generally solitary. And she'd

been so young. He should never have begun
the affair with her. Yet, she'd seemed happy.
Visiting her friends in neighbouring hamlets,
helping out in the inn when they were busy.

'We should have stayed in Bavaria,' he
murmured as he limped back to the bed.

'*I* should have stayed in Bavaria,' she corrected. 'But the accident might still have happened, mightn't it? And if you'd died, and I
hadn't been there...' Snuggling her head
tiredly onto his shoulder, she rested one hand
on his chest. 'I'm sorry I was so awful to you
when I was pregnant... I keep thinking about
how nasty I was.'

'Shh, you weren't nasty.'

Lifting her head, she gave him a wan smile.
'Yes, I was.' Resting her head back down,
she continued, 'I was thinking about it before
you came in. It seems such a long time ago,
almost a different life.' And if she'd been
able to see Jed immediately after the accident,
after she'd lost the baby, maybe the rift between them wouldn't have happened. But
he'd been in intensive care, and she'd been
very ill, and so it had been four days before
they'd been able to meet. Had she subconsciously blamed him for not being there to
comfort her? Had he blamed her? She didn't

even, really, know how he'd felt about the baby.

'You should ring your grandmother,' he said quietly. 'She's worried about you.'

'Yes, I'll ring her tomorrow.'

'You could go and stay with her...'

'No! No,' she denied more gently. She didn't want to leave him just now. She was afraid she might lose him if she did. The link between them seemed very tenuous at the moment, and she suspected she needed to be very careful. 'I'll start going for walks, get my strength back, eat properly. I could help you do your research...'

'One step at a time,' he cautioned. 'Get well first.'

'Yes.'

'I'm sorry about the baby, Sarah.'

'I know.'

Closing her eyes, she snuggled closer. She felt exhausted, sleepy, but her mind wouldn't settle. 'I didn't think I would be like this,' she whispered against him. 'So weak. Other people seem to cope with much worse...'

'Shh.'

But she didn't want to shh, she wanted to talk, explain how she felt, but maybe he didn't want that, maybe he just wanted to shut it out, forget it ever happened. And perhaps that would be best. But she couldn't forget. Every time she closed her eyes, it was there. She so vividly remembered the fear and the anguish of seeing him unconscious, blood running down his face, and then that awful pain in her insides, knowing, *knowing*, what was happening... If the parents of the child had gone immediately for an ambulance, not scrambled down and tried to help, maybe, maybe, she wouldn't have lost the baby...

Regulating his breathing to hers, he waited until she was asleep before gently extricating himself. Making sure she was warmly covered, he stared down at her for a few moments. She looked so vulnerable. With a deep sigh, he gathered up his clothing and quietly left.

Sarah woke once in the night, and cried softly when she found herself alone before slipping back into sleep, and when she woke in the morning she lay quietly for a few moments, just thinking, probing the wounds. The pain was still there, the sorrow, but she and Jed had made a small start at normality, hadn't they? She'd been selfish, she decided, selfish and stupid. It had been his baby too, of course he was hurting, feeling guilty, and she'd shut herself away because she'd been afraid to discuss it, afraid that he would say he was leaving. And who could blame him? She'd been a nightmare to live with, and now he probably felt responsible for her. Felt trapped.

And so she must get back to normal as quickly as possible, mustn't she? Get back to how she used to be. She would believe that he loved her, she decided, because anything else didn't bear contemplating, and if she pretended hard enough that everything was all right, then pretence would become reality, wouldn't it?

Feeling weak and a bit wobbly, she showered, dressed, and walked downstairs. Jed was cooking breakfast and she smiled at him, went to rest her head on his shoulder.

'Good morning.'

He smiled at her, a pale imitation of the way he used to smile, but a smile nevertheless. 'Egg and bacon,' he stated. Not a question.

She nodded and went to sit at the table. She ate most of it, drank her tea.

'What are you doing today?' she asked brightly. 'Writing?'

'Research, and then someone from the local paper is coming to interview me. What about you?'

'I shall go for a walk,' she said determinedly. He still wore a look of concern, and so she added, 'You mustn't worry about me any more, Jed. I'll be fine. Go on, go and do your research, I'll clear up the kitchen.'

'Sure?'

'Yes.'

He gave a small nod, kissed her forehead, and limped quietly along to his study and closed the door.

Allowing her smile to slip, her eyes to darken, she almost gave in to defeat. Almost, but then she took a deep breath and began to cheer up. She wouldn't believe it was hopeless. Rome wasn't built in a day, she assured herself. It would take time, and effort, but she would fight for him, fight to get everything back to normal.

When she was ready, she tapped on the study door, called that she wouldn't be long, and let herself out.

Clouds scudded along the sky, blown by a brisk wind, but it was no longer raining. Refusing to think about anything personal, she stared round her as though for the first time. The loch looked choppy, she decided,

the trees skeletal. And those poor sheep hud-
dled on the hillside looked as miserable as
sin. Think *happy* thoughts, Sarah, think pos-
itive, she told herself. Brisk striding was out
because she simply didn't have the energy,
but if Jed could get to the crossroads with his
bad leg, then so could she.

It took her a long time, with frequent rests,
but she made it, and then went further as
though needing to prove something to herself.
She knew there was a village up ahead, and
maybe they had a coffee shop where she
could rest before going back. There was the
school where, presumably, the boy she had
spoken to went, and then the village street.
Granite houses gave way to a small row of
shops. A butcher's, greengrocer's, even a
hairdresser's, but no coffee shop. There was
even a war memorial, and she stood beside it
for a while to read the names and rest.

When she was ready, she walked slowly
back to the house, and over the next few days
she continued to exercise, continued to eat,
but she and Jed were no closer. They talked,
smiled at each other, but there was still a barrier between them that she didn't know how
to bridge. He still slept in the spare room—
because he didn't want to disturb her with his

restlessness, he said. If there were kisses, she was the one who instigated them, and then, on the Friday, his friends came—the ones who were having the anniversary party the following week.

She was in the kitchen when they came, and so Jed let them in. She heard them talking, laughing, heard the sounds of long friendship, and so she pinned a smile to her face and walked out to join them.

'This is Sarah,' Jed said quietly. 'My wife.'

The shock on both their faces halted her.

'Oh, my goodness!' the woman exclaimed faintly. 'We thought, I mean…'

'That we'd imagined you differently,' her husband put in quickly. He was a big, amiable-looking man, his wife slender, elegant, with a mobile face. 'We knew Jed was married—not that he invited us to the wedding.' He reproved Jed with a look. 'But you know how you get in your mind an image of how someone will be…' Taking a deep breath, he grinned at her, a grin that looked suspiciously false to Sarah. 'I'm Duncan, and this is my wife, Fiona. We're very pleased to meet you.'

Hurrying forward, Fiona clasped her shoulders and kissed her on both cheeks. 'Of course we are. Don't take any notice of us,

we've been away and the journey back was a
nightmare. Haven't even been home yet.
Shall we start again?'

'Yes.' Sarah smiled. 'It's nice to meet you
both. Jed said you'd been friends a long
time.'

'Yes,' Fiona agreed with a fond smile for
Jed. 'Of course, we knew him before he was
famous,' she teased and he pulled a face.

'I'll go and put the coffee on,' he began,
but Sarah quickly touched his arm and
smiled.

'I'll do it. You all go into the lounge.'
Hurrying back to the kitchen, she filled the
kettle and put it on to boil. Why had they
been so surprised? she wondered. Almost as
if they'd been expecting someone else. But
who—? Not that she was intending to ask. Jed
didn't seem to like being asked questions,
and, at the moment, with everything being so
shaky between them she didn't want any
more points of contention. Putting everything
on a tray, she carried it through and then sat
beside Fiona on the sofa.

'Tell me about you,' Fiona encouraged
with a friendly smile. 'We knew Jed was married, of course—not from your wretched husband, I might add, which I don't intend to

forgive him for, but from my mother. We've been spending the festive season with some friends in London, and when I rang to tell her when we'd be back she said Jed was here and that he was married! And when I asked who he was married to, she said wait and see! Which wasn't very helpful. I was never more shocked in my life! In his last letter, he never even hinted that he was thinking of getting wed. How long have you known each other?'

'Since last May.'

'A whirlwind romance.' Fiona smiled. 'How exciting, and I'm so pleased for Jed. It was time he settled down.'

'Yes,' Sarah agreed inadequately. Glancing at him, seeing him in animated conversation with Duncan, she wanted to cry again. He looked like he used to look; complete, sure of himself. Amused.

'You love him very much, don't you?' Fiona asked softly.

'Yes.' And it was breaking her heart. Forcing a smile, she asked, 'And you? It's your fifth anniversary, isn't it?'

'Yes. Any excuse for a party, I always say. You will come, won't you?' she pleaded. 'Everyone so wants to see Jed again—and you, of course. Mum said you weren't well

after the accident, and Jed's leg is still painful, but even if you only come for an hour or
so... Please say you will.'

'It's up to Jed...' Sarah began, only to be
overruled.

'No, it isn't. It's up to you. Men always do
as they're told.' Fiona laughed. 'Just tell him
you want to go. Please?'

'Jed can go...'

'No, that's no good. He won't come without you. Will you, Jed?' she called across.
When he looked up, she smiled at him. 'I'm
trying to persuade your lovely Sarah to come
to our party, because you won't come without
her, will you? Not that we want you to,' she
added hastily, 'but you *must* come.'

'Must I?' he asked with a faint smile.
Glancing at his wife, he added, 'We'll see
how Sarah feels next week.'

'Feel better,' Fiona urged her. 'You'll enjoy it. We're all very nice.'

'It isn't that...'

'I know. But do try, please?'

'Leave the poor girl alone,' Duncan put in.
'You're embarrassing her. Jed said you
paint,' he commented gently.

'Now who's being embarrassing?' Fiona
enquired archly.

Sarah gave a faint smile. 'I'm not very good…'

'Yes, you are,' Jed said quietly.

'And there speaks the proud husband.' Fiona laughed, and then she looked at her husband, pleaded softly, 'Can I tell them? I have to tell *someone*, I'm almost bursting with it.' Duncan gave her a fond smile, and she announced boldly, 'I'm pregnant!'

Almost uncomprehending for a moment, Sarah just stared at her, and it was left to Jed to leap into the sudden silence. He got up, pulled Fiona to her feet and gave her a hug. 'I'm so pleased,' he said softly, sincerely. 'Well done.' Turning to Duncan, he shook his hand and then went to perch beside Sarah, put his arm round her shoulders and gave them an unobtrusive squeeze. 'They've been trying for a long time to have a baby,' he explained, and his voice sounded rough, slightly husky.

'And spending a fortune to do so.' Duncan laughed, clearly as delighted as his wife. 'It will be the most expensive baby on record.'

Still smiling, Fiona resumed her seat. 'IVF,' she explained to Sarah. 'We were beginning to think it would never work. But now…'

Grateful for Jed's arm round her, leaning slightly into him, shutting out every thought, every emotion, she focused solely on Fiona. 'I'm so pleased for you,' Sarah murmured. 'Will it be a multiple birth?'

'No,' she denied, 'just the one. So, you see, you must come to our party. We have so much to celebrate.'

'Then of course we will come,' she made herself say. Determined not to spoil Fiona and Duncan's pleasure, she smiled at them both. 'Of course we will come,' she repeated. She had promised herself she would change, break out of her depression, and going to a party would help, wouldn't it?

'Is your mother well?' Jed broke in. 'I've been meaning to go and see her.'

'And never got around to it, yes, I know. But, yes, she's fine, we'll pop in on our way home to tell her our news. I didn't want to tell her over the phone. I still can't believe it,' Fiona whispered. 'I have to keep pinching myself to make sure it's true, that next July, God willing, we'll be parents.'

And if God had been willing for herself, then she and Jed would have been parents in May. But He hadn't been willing, and so she must finally put it behind her. On impulse,

Sarah leaned forward and kissed Fiona's cheek. 'Well done—and take very good care of yourself.'

'I will, and thank you.' Glancing at her husband, she smiled. 'We'd better go, Mum will wonder where we've got to.'

Jed saw them out, and when he returned to the lounge Sarah was standing at the window staring out. 'We should send Fiona some flowers,' Sarah began.

'Yes. Are you all right? If I'd known—'

'No,' she broke in. 'People have babies all the time, I can't pretend they don't exist. I'm very pleased for them. I liked them.'

'They liked you too.'

Had they? That was nice, and once, she thought sadly, Jed had liked her. He would have walked up behind her, put his arms round her and rested his chin on her hair. But that obviously wasn't going to happen, was it? And so she must pretend that she had noticed nothing amiss. Turning, she gave him a forced smile. 'Are *you* all right?'

'Yes. Are you sure you want to go to the party?'

'Yes,' she said firmly. 'I think it will do us good.'

'Well, we'll see how you feel.'

Didn't he want to go? she wondered as she watched him collect up the coffee-cups to take into the kitchen. Or did he not want her to go? Not so long ago she would have plagued him with questions, but plaguing him with questions was the old Sarah; the new Sarah wasn't going to plague him at all.

The week slipped by without fuss, without drama. Jed was working again, or, at least, he was shutting himself in his study every day, and she continued her walks. It was colder now. Mrs Reeves had even prophesied snow, but Sarah still walked as far as the village, or up on the hills. Determined to make an effort, she'd had her hair cut and styled, driven into the nearest town for a long black skirt and top, and now she was as ready as she was ever going to be for the party.

'You look nice,' Jed said quietly as she walked downstairs.

'Thank you, so do you.'

He gave a small smile.

His mother had been a Scot, and so, she supposed, he could be called a Celt. Or half of one, at any rate. Fine-boned with those amazing green eyes that always looked so startling, he would have made an excellent Heathcliff. A very smart Heathcliffe at the moment. She was more used to seeing him in jeans or cords—he looked unfamiliar in his jacket and tie and well-cut grey trousers. Sarah thought she would have liked to have seen him in a kilt, but when she'd asked he'd merely shaken his head.

Helping her on with her thick coat, he shrugged into his own old sheepskin and carefully escorted her down the steep steps. 'Careful,' he cautioned. 'I did put salt on them but they still feel icy.'

Clutching the rail tighter because they didn't want any more accidents, she murmured, 'Mrs Reeves thought it might snow.'

'Too cold.'

Opening the car door for her, he helped her inside, then limped round to climb in beside her. He was walking better, but she didn't comment. As she didn't comment on so many things now.

They were like strangers, and he seemed more tense than usual. Right up until yesterday he hadn't thought they should go, and then, suddenly, this morning, he had changed his mind.

It was only a half-hour drive, and when they pulled up outside a large old house and he switched off the engine he suddenly turned to her. 'Sarah…'

But whatever he'd been going to say was lost as the front door of the house was flung open and both Fiona and Duncan hurried out to greet them.

They were ushered quickly inside out of the cold, their coats were taken and they were propelled into a very large room decorated with fir and spruce. A fire crackled warmly in a large fireplace and candlelight augmented the overhead light which had been dimmed.

Sarah didn't miss the curious glances she received as they were introduced to the people already there. Neither did she miss seeing the rather querulous old lady sitting in a corner who had been imperiously trying to catch Fiona's attention for the past five minutes.

'I think someone is trying…' Sarah began hesitantly, and Fiona grimaced.

'Great Aunt Jane,' she explained with a downturned mouth. 'My grandmother's younger sister. Oh, well, best get it over with. And, Sarah, please don't take any notice of what she says; she can be a bit blunt… She's also a bit deaf and tends to shout.' She glanced at Jed as if for help, and when none was forthcoming she sighed and led Sarah and Jed over to her great aunt.

'Aunt, this is—'

'Where's Deanna?' Great Aunt Jane broke in.

'Deanna isn't here...'

'Of course she must be here. Jed is. You said he was married.'

'He is,' Fiona continued in exasperation. 'To—'

'Then where is she? I might be going deaf but there's nothing wrong with my brain.' Turning to Jed, she said almost accusingly, 'Certainly took your time about it. In my day we knew what we wanted and went for it, and why are you limping?'

'I was in a car crash...'

'Hmph, always did drive too fast, and your hair needs cutting; you look like a gypsy. Where is she, then?'

'I have no idea,' he dismissed quietly. 'I didn't marry Deanna, I married Sarah.' Putting his hand against Sarah's back, he added firmly, 'This Sarah.'

She looked Sarah up and down and dismissed her. 'Catch you, did she?' she asked maliciously. 'Oldest trick in the—'

'Aunt!' Fiona broke in in embarrassment. 'Don't be so rude.'

'I liked Deanna,' she stated firmly. 'She made me laugh, and why haven't I got a drink?'

'I'll get you one,' Jed offered quietly.

'No, you won't, I want to talk to you. Fiona, you get it and take this girl with you.' With an impatient shushing motion to the two women, she patted the seat beside her and bade Jed sit. Only Jed wasn't to be bade. He held her gaze for long moments, and then said firmly, 'I'll come and see you later.' Turning away, he took Sarah's arm. 'Come on, let's get a drink.'

Aware that everyone in the room must have heard the old lady's words, she allowed herself to be led. From utter silence, animated conversation suddenly broke out, and she tilted her chin just a little bit higher.

'Who's Deanna?' she asked softly, and with just the slightest hint of temper.

'Someone I used to go out with. I'm sorry, I stupidly thought everyone would have forgotten.'

No, she thought sadly, he'd hoped everyone would have been too well-bred to have mentioned it. Hoped, perhaps, that Fiona

would have warned everyone in advance not
to say anything.

'What will you have to drink?'

'White wine.'

When it had been put into her hand and
they'd moved a little way away from the bar,
she murmured without looking at him, 'When
Duncan and Fiona came last week, they expected to see Deanna, didn't they?'

'I don't know.'

'Yes, you do. Were you in love with her?'

'I don't remember.'

'Don't lie, Jed,' she pleaded tiredly.
'Please don't lie.'

CHAPTER FOUR

'I'M NOT. I don't know if I was in love with her. When I first met her, I was attracted, bemused perhaps, but love? I don't know. It's over a year since I last saw her; a lot has happened since then.' Staring down into the mineral water he'd opted for because he was driving, he absently swirled it round and round. 'We met at Fiona and Duncan's wedding. Fiona and I were at school together, we'd kept in touch over the years and she invited me to her wedding.' There was a small disturbance by the door as some new arrivals entered, and he broke off, glanced towards them, and gave a faint smile. It looked incredibly cynical. A tall, thin man with sandy hair suddenly spotted him and strode across.

'Jed, you old rascal! How are you? And where's the delectable Deanna? Someone said you were married. I didn't believe it, of course... What? Jed? I said. The old adventurer? Rubbish. Jed's not the marrying kind, I told them. My God, you're the one we all envied! Doing what you like, going where you like; domesticity was never for you... But then, if you had to get married, I suppose Deanna was your best bet. She's as adventurous as you are.' Belatedly becoming aware of Sarah, he turned to her, gave a wide grin. 'Sorry to butt in—Jed and I are old friends. Angus,' he introduced himself with a thrust-out hand.

'Sarah,' she smiled as she shook it. And, really rather fed up with being treated as a nonentity, added, 'Jed's wife.'

'Sorry?' he queried with a rather blank look. 'Thought for a minute you said you were his wife.'

'I did. He didn't marry Deanna.'

He went red, coughed, started to speak, changed his mind, and said inadequately, 'Oh.'

'Don't worry about it,' she said with an amiability that might have scraped paint.

'No. I'm very pleased to meet you. Really,' he insisted, his face even redder. 'Just that I assumed... Sorry. Women hated her, men loved her,' he rushed on making bad worse. 'Outgoing, outrageous and the most shocking flirt you ever met.' Turning to Jed in desperation, he asked, 'Did you ever hear what happened to her?'

'No,' he denied quietly. 'So, what are you up to these days? Still with the Embassy?'

'Yes, I—'

'Would you excuse me?' Sarah broke in. 'I need to powder my nose.' With a small, rather meaningless smile, she put her glass down and made for the doorway. People looked embarrassed as she passed them, and she forced herself to keep smiling.

Gaining the sanctuary of the downstairs cloakroom, fortunately empty, she slipped inside and locked the door. Staring at herself in the mirror, her teeth slightly gritted, she wondered if that was why Jed had been reluctant to come. Because he'd known that everyone was going to compare her to Deanna? Why *hadn't* he married her? Clearly everyone expected he should have done. Except Angus, of course. Outgoing and outrageous, he'd said. And she'd been like that. Once. Before she'd got pregnant. And then she'd changed, and so had Jed.

Did Deanna live in Scotland? Had he been hoping to see her again? He hadn't intended for Sarah to come, had he? She was the one who had insisted she be with him. She knew so little about his life before they met. She knew he'd been a foreign correspondent for

one of the London television companies'
newsdesks, that he'd been sickened by the
wars he'd covered, knew that he was passion-
ately interested in European history and that
his knowledge of one particular incident had
turned into the first of his best-selling novels,
but she didn't know anything of his life here.

Someone rattled the door handle, and she
jumped.

'Coming,' she called. Taking a deep breath,
she turned to open the door—and overheard a
conversation. So involved in their gossip, the
two middle-aged women didn't even look up
to see that the door had been unlatched, and
so continued, oblivious to Sarah's presence.

'Poor girl, she clearly had no idea about
Deanna. You'd think Jed might have warned
her.'

'No, you wouldn't!' the other woman answered drily. 'Men don't like confrontations.
What was she like?'

'Deanna? Oh, tall, red hair, and the most
amazing eyes you ever saw. Bluey grey.
Animated, she was, alive, a flirt, of course, had
men round her like bees round a honey pot.
But that was Deanna. Not that we thought he
would ever get married to her, or anyone else

come to that. He wasn't the type. I mean, you can't imagine Jed with *babies*, can you?'

'Oh, I don't know. Rather a moody-looking devil, isn't he?'

'Mmm, brooding and solitary, or so we all thought. Sexiest man on the planet, someone once dubbed him.' With a small smile, and presumably remembering she was outside the cloakroom for a reason, she looked up, stared straight into Sarah's face, and went scarlet. 'Oh, my dear,' she began awkwardly. 'We weren't... I mean, we didn't...'

'It's all right,' Sarah managed with a smile. 'I think he's pretty sexy too. Sorry I was so long,' she added quietly, and walked back to the main room.

'You didn't know about her, did you?'

Startled, she turned to face Fiona. About to lie, she suddenly changed her mind. 'No,' she denied softly.

'Want some advice?' Fiona asked gently, and then gave it without waiting for Sarah to answer. 'Don't nag him about it. Don't make more of it than there is.'

'No,' she agreed, 'but then, it's none of my business, is it? It all happened before we even met.'

'And you aren't even *curious*?' Fiona asked in disbelief.

'Oh, yes, I'm curious—who wouldn't be?'

'She wasn't very nice sometimes...'

'You don't know that I am,' Sarah pointed out.

'Yes, I do. Jed wouldn't have married you otherwise.'

And probably wouldn't have married her at all if it hadn't been for the baby.

'I'm sorry about Great Aunt Jane,' Fiona continued quietly. 'I think she's going a bit senile.'

'It's all right,' Sarah reassured her. 'I had to find out some time. Don't let it spoil your party, and I have to tell you,' she managed to tease, 'that I am very disappointed that no one is wearing the kilt.'

'Come to one of our formal bashes,' Fiona invited in relief. 'Everyone wears them then.'

'Including Jed?'

'I don't think Jed has one. You'll have to persuade him. He would look fantastic. That man has very nice legs!'

'How do you know?'

Fiona laughed. 'Now, that would be telling! No, seriously, we were at school together. I used to see him playing rugby, and if he was

up here in the summer we'd often go swimming.'

Along with Deanna? Wearing a minuscule
bikini? But she wouldn't ask, and as someone
came up to talk to Fiona she slipped away to
find Jed. He was sitting chatting to Mrs
McKenzie, Fiona's mother, and she walked to
join them.

He smiled up at her, and got up to give her
his seat. 'All right?'

'Yes, I'm fine.'

'We'll go soon.'

She gave a small nod. 'Would you get my
drink for me, please?'

'Yes, of course.' He walked away and
Fiona's mother said softly. 'I think this is all
my fault. I should have told Fiona in the beginning who Jed was married to.'

'But it wasn't only Fiona, was it?'

'No,' she agreed. 'But I do wish you both
happiness. I like Jed.'

'So do I.'

Taking Sarah by surprise, she reached
across and warmly clasped one of Sarah's
hands. 'You've not been well, I hear.'

'No. Just the after-effects of the car crash.
I'm much better now.'

'And it took an awful lot of courage to

come here tonight, didn't it?' she asked sympathetically. 'No, no need to answer, and it's done now. People will now see you as yourself. Tell me what you do. You'll need some occupation, won't you, when Jed's writing?'

'Yes. When we were in Bavaria, a lovely little village not far from Oberammergau, where they hold the Passion Play,' she explained in case that made it clearer, 'I used to help out in the inn when they were busy; visit my friends…' It sounded very lame. 'I'd only just finished at college, was taking a year off before looking for a job…'

'And then you met Jed.'

'Yes.' Remembering that day, she gave a small smile.

'Tell me about Bavaria. I've never been there.'

'Oh, balconied chalets that are garlanded in summer, music. Always music. Brass bands, cowbells,' she added with another smile. 'Rococo and baroque churches. Skiing in winter, hot sunny days in summer. It's very— *Gemütlich*.'

'Which means?' Mrs McKenzie asked drily.

'Comfortable; friendly—but you're right, I will need something to do.'

'Fiona said you paint.'

With a deprecating smile, she murmured, 'Sometimes.'

'And sold all her work to tourists in Bavaria,' Jed put in. 'She's an excellent painter,' he informed Mrs McKenzie as he handed Sarah her drink. 'You should get her to paint your portrait.'

She stared at Sarah with interest, sipped at her own drink for a few minutes in silence, and then asked, 'Will you?' And then she chuckled. 'Now, wouldn't that be a nice surprise for Fiona?' she asked with dry humour. 'We could start a family portrait gallery.' Eyes brightening, she gave an enthusiastic nod. 'Come and see me. Jed knows where I live.'

Slightly alarmed, Sarah warned, 'I'm not a professional or anything...'

'But a gifted amateur?'

'Yes,' Jed insisted.

Sarah glanced rather worriedly at her husband, and then back to Mrs McKenzie, and then, almost to her surprise, she felt a tiny spurt of enthusiasm. 'All right,' she agreed. 'I will.'

'Good. Now take the lassie home, Jed. She's borne enough for one evening.'

He smiled, bent to kiss her and helped Sarah to her feet.

Five minutes later they'd said their good-
byes and were out in the cold night air. 'I'm
sorry,' he apologised quietly.

'It's all right.'

'You have every right to be angry.'

'Yes,' she agreed. 'It wasn't very nice being
compared to someone else, and found wanting.'

'You weren't…'

'Yes, Jed, I was,' she insisted firmly. 'Are
there any other dark secrets I should know
about?'

'Deanna wasn't a dark secret, and, no, there
isn't anything else you should know.'

Watching her breath cloud the frosty air, she
added quietly, 'I'm only just beginning to discover how little I know about you. About your
life before we met.'

'You only have to ask…'

'But you don't *like* being asked questions!'
she interrupted.

He looked astonished. 'I don't?'

'No. Well,' she qualified, 'you don't look
as though you do. You grew up here, didn't
you?'

'From the age of eleven to sixteen. I went
to the local school. Mother and I even stayed,
for a while, in the house where we live.'

'Oh,' she said inadequately. 'Were you happy?'

'No,' he denied simply, and then he gave a small, self-mocking smile. 'I was stoical.'

He still was. 'And your mother? What was she like?'

'Even more stoical,' he said drily. 'Do you mind doing Mrs McKenzie's portrait?'

'No,' she denied. 'If you think I'm good enough.'

'I do.' Taking her hand warmly in his, he gently squeezed it. For a moment she felt safe and warm again, and she leaned gratefully against his shoulder.

'It will be nice to have something to do.'

'Yes.' Helping her into the car, he passed her the seat belt and gently closed the door. His footsteps crunched on the icy gravel as he walked round to his own seat and the sound was comforting, familiar. It was going to be all right, she assured herself. Deanna was history; she had to stay there.

Sleepily watching the hedgerows as they passed, she turned her head obediently when Jed pointed out Mrs McKenzie's house. A square, no-nonsense sort of place, and she smiled. She would need to buy materials, a sketch-pad, pencils, paints… A formal picture, she decided, as a start to the rogue's gallery. She could almost see it at the head of the stairs, and below it would hang Fiona, or maybe Fiona and Duncan...

'I like it when it's like this,' Jed murmured quietly. 'Silent, no traffic, a winter landscape. We could almost be at the beginning of the last century.'

'A stagecoach,' Sarah put in, 'racing through the night. Horse's breath pluming, the crack of the whip as the driver urges them on towards safety.'

'The passengers jostled, bruised, luggage bouncing on the roof...'

'And then a lone figure, with a masked face, his pistols raised. Stand and deliver. I wonder if they really said that?' Sarah mused.

'I wonder.'

'I imagine it would have been safer to have fired a warning shot before they were run down. Four horses plunging recklessly through the night would be hard to stop, I imagine.'

'No, no,' he denied humorously, 'the driver is excellent, totally in control.'

She chuckled, imagining it, the racket they must have made. 'And does your hero solve the murder in your book?'

'Oh, aye.' He smiled. 'He solves it. I don't

know *how* yet, but he will solve it. And here we are, safely home.'

He parked the car in the small garage and even put his arm round her to help her up the steep steps and indoors. He'd left the hall light burning and the heating on, so it felt warm and safe.

'A nightcap?' he asked her as he hung up his coat and helped her off with hers. 'Hot milk? Chocolate?'

'Chocolate.' Turning towards him in the small hall, she smiled, reached up to kiss his cold mouth, and this time he didn't pull away, but kissed her gently back. He didn't prolong the kiss, but he did smile at her before ushering her towards the stairs.

'I'll bring it up to you. Go and get into bed.'

She nodded, felt suddenly breathless, a small leap of excitement. Did he intend to stay with her? But she couldn't ask, *wouldn't* ask, just accept until everything was back to normal. Which wouldn't be long, she prayed. Not long at all.

She was in bed with the pillows stacked behind her and the quilt drawn up under her arms when he came up with her hot chocolate. He placed it carefully on the bedside table, and then perched on the edge of the bed.

'Talking in the car gave me some ideas I want to get down whilst I think of them.' He smiled. 'So drink your chocolate, then snuggle down and get some sleep. And thank you for tonight.' Leaning forward, he kissed her gently on the nose, squeezed her hand, and walked out.

As the door closed softly behind him, she continued to stare blankly at it. She was glad he had some ideas at last, really she was, but... Was he feeling relieved that he had an excuse not to stay with her? He was behaving like a brother, or an uncle, and she wanted a husband. Couldn't he see that? Or didn't he want to? Maybe he thought the evening had been too much for her. Or maybe he wanted to be on his own to think about Deanna. Don't nag him about it, Fiona had said. *Why* had she said that? Because it was a touchy subject and everyone knew that he was still in love with her?

'No,' she said aloud. 'I won't have this. I won't.' Picking up her chocolate, she slowly drank half of it and then turned out the light and snuggled down. Should she force the issue, or let sleeping dogs lie? But Deanna wasn't sleeping, was she? She'd been resurrected, and Sarah had no idea what to do for the best.

Sleep on it, she thought. Sleeping, the subconscious often worked things out. Disappointed, lonely, she closed her eyes and tried to capture sleep, but all she could see was Jed and a tall, red-haired girl. Laughing together, swimming together... Sleeping together? She supposed they had, if they'd been in love. But he'd slept with herself *after* Deanna, and it had been good, hadn't it? And would be again. Sarah, you think too much, go to sleep.

She slept fitfully, her mind continually picturing Jed with Deanna, but when she woke in the morning to find Jed standing beside her with a cup of tea she forced all thoughts of Deanna aside and smiled at him.

Scrambling up in the bed, she took her tea and said, 'This is a nice surprise.'

'Good.' Perching on the edge of the bed, he asked quietly, 'How did you sleep?'

'Fine,' she lied.

'Feel up to going out for the day? I thought we might drive into Glasgow, have some lunch, look for painting materials...'

'I'd like that.'

He smiled and got to his feet. 'I'll go and

get the breakfast going. It looks like it might snow,' he added as he walked to the door, 'so dress appropriately.'

The sky was a yellowy, leaden colour as they set off, with absolutely no wind. Sarah opened her window slightly and took a deep breath. 'Smells like snow,' she commented knowledgeably, and he gave a small smile.

They didn't talk very much on the journey, but she was content merely to be beside him. Although she'd been to Glasgow before, she hadn't seen anything of the city. When she'd arrived, it had been by ambulance, and when she'd left, she hadn't been in any fit state to notice very much. Looking interestedly round her as they entered the outskirts, she gave a small smile as she recognised the names of some of the places they passed. Maryhill, Kelvinside, Partick Thistle Football Club, and, as they entered the city proper, she exclaimed in surprise, 'It's really rather elegant, isn't it?'

'Glasgow? Yes, it's a city I've always liked. It means Dear Green Place.'

'Glasgow does?' she asked in astonishment. 'Green?'

'Mmm, and there are still green places if

you know where to look. Parks, open
squares…'

'You lived here at one time?'

'No, but I used to come in on the bus,' he
volunteered. 'Evenings, weekends…'

'From where we live now?' she asked in
surprise.

'Yes.'

'It must have taken for ever!'

He gave a small smile. 'It did. Went round
every village and hamlet.'

'And then what?' she asked curiously.

'Oh, I'd wander round…'

'By yourself?'

'Yes. I'd visit the markets, do my home-
work in the library, ask questions,' he added
softly. 'I think I was a little in love with the
librarian. Miss Dewar. I was all of twelve.'

Watching his face as he scanned the busy
roads for a parking space, she gave a small,
fond smile. She could so easily imagine him
as a boy, dark hair flopping over his face; how
he would impatiently shove it back. Intense,
solitary. 'Were you intense?' she asked softly.

'Oh, yes.' Sparing her a glance, he grinned.
'Very serious, very solemn.'

'And clever?'

'Maybe.'

'Tell me about Miss Dewar.'

He gave a soft laugh. 'Oh, she was maybe twenty-four, twenty-five...'

'Pretty?'

'No-o,' he denied slowly, 'not pretty, but she was kind, gentle. She never made me feel I was being a nuisance. Lord, the questions I used to ask—ah, finally, a space.' Swinging quickly into the vacant spot, he turned to smile at her.

She smiled back. 'I wish I'd known you then.'

'No, you don't,' he denied. 'I didn't like girls.'

'Only Miss Dewar.'

'Yes. Come on. Lunch first and then we'll find you an art shop.'

They ate in a little Italian restaurant, and it was almost like old times. Seemingly relaxed for the first time in weeks, he told her a little about his boyhood, about helping out in the markets to earn pocket money. About how he used to watch people, listen to what they said. 'I thought myself very grown up, very—so-phisticated,' he added with a wry, self-mocking smile.

'And was Fiona your *only* friend?' she

asked in surprise. She couldn't imagine only having one friend.

'Only because she would persist in following me around as though she were my keeper.'

'In which case, you wouldn't have had *any*?'

'Don't sound so shocked.' He laughed. 'I *liked* my own company. Still do.'

'But didn't you go out to play?' she asked in perplexed bewilderment. 'Have adventures? Break windows? Play football?'

Eyes amused, he shook his head. 'You find it incomprehensible?'

'Well, yes. I belonged to a gang.'

His lips twitched.

'Not a nasty gang or anything, but we used to go snake-hunting, and mountaineering, make *camps*. We'd get dirty and hungry and…'

'And you kept in touch with these childhood chums?'

'Some of them, yes. You sound so *deprived*!' she exclaimed worriedly.

'And that bothers you?' he asked gently.

'Yes.'

'It was a long time ago…'

'I know, but…'

He smiled, patted her hand. 'Come on, let's go and find this art shop.'

Vaguely troubled by a childhood she didn't understand, she watched him whilst he paid the bill, and then walked with him out into the cold.

Hurrying her along until she began to laugh in protest, his hand warmly clasping hers, he dragged her into the precinct out of the wind and led her to a small shop. Glancing at his watch, he asked, 'Can I leave you to select all you need whilst I nip to the library?'

'To see Miss Dewar?' she teased, and he smiled.

'Who knows? I won't be long.'

'OK.'

He kissed her and disappeared. Because he liked his own company? she wondered. Because being with her for more than an hour or so... Stop it, she told herself fiercely. Why on earth do you have to keep *imagining* things? Why can't you just take as you find? Because it mattered, that was why.

'Need some help?'

Swinging round, she stared at the shop assistant. A young man with an eager face.

'You look a little bewildered.'

'Oh, yes, sorry. I need some paints, and

things,' she added vaguely. Pulling herself together, and with the help of the assistant, she
began choosing her materials. It didn't take
very long, not nearly the hour and half Jed was
away. Beginning to get worried, she gave a
sigh of relief when he hurried in.

'Sarah, I'm sorry,' he apologised. 'I found
a bookshop…'

'Say no more,' she said with a smile.
'Bookshops, I know about.'

Eyes amused, grateful perhaps, he turned to
look at the rather small stack of items she'd
collected and frowned. 'Won't you need an
easel?'

Embarrassed in case the sales assistant
should overhear, she whispered, 'They're a bit
expensive. I thought I could tack the canvas
to a board…'

'You will not. If something is worth doing,
it's worth doing properly. Come on.' Taking
her arm, he ushered her round the shop, and
by the time they'd finished the pile on the
counter had grown alarmingly.

'Jed, it's going to cost a fortune!' she protested.

'So? When was the last time I spent anything on you?' he asked almost fiercely. 'This
is something I can do, Sarah, so let me do it.'

Watching him as he paid for everything, she felt bewildered, and guilty, and wondered why she should feel either. But she didn't like him paying for her own things because she felt as though she didn't give anything back. Did other wives feel like that? she wondered.

'Stop looking so worried,' he reproved. 'People will think I'm forcing you to take up art. I'm not, am I?' he asked softly. 'I did rather pitch you into this.'

'No, you didn't! I want to do it, it just seems a lot of money to spend on me. I don't expect you to do all these things for me, Jed.'

'I know,' he agreed almost grimly, and then, almost under his breath, added, 'I think that's half the trouble.'

'Sorry?'

'Nothing. Call it a late Christmas present.'

'I didn't buy you anything,' she said sadly. But then, she didn't have very much money left, not after buying her outfit for the party. And Christmas had been spent with Jed in the hospital.

'Let's take these back to the car,' he said more briskly, 'and then we'll go and have a coffee. Any other shopping you want to do whilst you're here? Winter clothing? Snow boots?'

She shook her head.

The shop assistant, not having a bag big enough, had put everything into a large plastic bin-liner, and as Jed hoisted the unwieldy mass into his arms, waited for her to open the door for him, he suddenly halted and looked down into her big brown eyes. 'Don't you know...?' he began softly, and then pulled a face. 'Never mind, come on.'

When they'd had their coffee and a casual stroll round the pedestrianised shopping centre it was beginning to get dark, and colder. Her gloved hands tucked warmly into his arm, she rested her head against his shoulder. Women watched him as they passed, tried to catch his eye, but he was hers. For now, he was hers. A tall, vitally attractive man who had that certain something that women found impossible to resist.

'Tired?'

'A bit,' she confessed. But happier than she had been for a long time, and a little bit sad. But then, February always seemed a sad month, and without a Christmas to look back on... Glancing up at the street lamps, she saw a lone snowflake drift past. Time to go home.

By the time they reached the open countryside, the snow was coming down harder. Big, fat flakes that settled on the windscreen and were impacted by the wipers, and the further they drove, the whiter everything became.

'The ski lodges will be pleased,' Jed commented as he turned the heater up another notch. 'I expect they're praying we'll have enough to give them a good season.'

'And this time last year, we hadn't even met.'

'No.'

'I always meant to learn to ski. You do, don't you? Sorry,' she hastily added as she remembered his leg and that he might not now be able to ski at all. 'That was insensitive. I didn't mean...'

'It's not your fault, Sarah.'

'But it is,' she said miserably. And they had to talk about it, didn't they? Not keep shutting it out. 'Was I driving too fast?' she asked quietly.

'No, and we have to look forward, Sarah, not continually hark back to the past.'

'But we don't, do we? We don't mention it at all.'

'Because nothing will change it,' he said almost impatiently, 'and post-mortems are a waste of time.'

'It might help us to understand it...'

'No.'

With a deep sigh, she burst out, 'You are so—intransigent!'

'Yes,' he agreed.

'Yes,' she mimicked. 'Because you don't like other people very much, do you? You like to be alone! You don't like being questioned!' She wanted to hit him. 'I sometimes think it would be easier if you shouted at me. Blamed me…'

'There's nothing to blame.'

'Yes, there is!' she cried. 'I *need* to be blamed, need to atone—'

'Don't be absurd,' he cut in almost harshly. 'It was an accident! And now is not the time to discuss it.'

'Then when will be the time?' she demanded. 'Every time I bring it up, you avoid it, refuse to talk about it…'

'And you don't?'

'No, yes… It's because—'

'Because what?' he interrupted. 'What is it because?'

Suddenly frightened at where this might be taking them, afraid to ask, afraid he would say what she so desperately didn't want him to say, she backed off. 'Nothing, I don't know,' she mumbled.

'Then there's no *point* to this, is there?' Hands tight on the wheel, he took a deep breath, eased his foot slightly on the accelerator. 'There's no point,' he repeated. 'It happened, and now it's over and done with. If you really feel the need to talk…'

'See a psychiatrist?' she asked bitterly, and cursed herself for her too-ready tongue.

He said something under his breath, then pulled carefully onto the hard shoulder and stopped. Turning to face her, he said quietly, 'I'm sorry. I know I'm not being much help, but…'

'You don't want to talk about it, do you?'

'No,' he agreed simply, 'and I don't think you do either. Not yet. I don't think you're ready for it, Sarah. When you're better, stronger…'

Less emotional? Perhaps he was right. Afraid to make an issue of it, afraid of angering him, alienating him, she swallowed and finally nodded. 'I expect you're right.' Forcing a smile, she added much too brightly, 'We'd better get going before we get stuck in the snow.'

'Yes.' He looked for a moment as though he might say something else, and then he turned away, switched the ignition back on and pulled carefully back onto the road. 'When will you start your painting?' he asked carefully.

'Oh, Monday, I expect.' Feeling despair and hopelessness, she forced them down, tried to make her voice as pleasant as his, but it wasn't going to go away, was it? If they never discussed it, explained how they were feeling, how would they ever resolve it? Get close again? It would bubble away under the surface until... No, she was determined, that wouldn't happen. If he didn't want to talk about it, *couldn't* talk about it, then she must respect his wishes, but, oh, how she wished he would just tell her things. Perhaps he had never learned how. He was too used to being solitary... But all she wanted to know was that he loved her, wasn't it? Nothing else. 'Jed,' she began as she tried to formulate a question that might help her to understand his feelings, and then changed her mind. Perhaps now was not the time. Not when he was driving. Not when she was upset. 'What did you find in the bookshop?' she asked instead.

He smiled in obvious relief, and clearly making an effort, as she was, he explained with false enthusiasm, 'An excellent little book about Queen Victoria's Scotland. That's why I was so long. I was so busy reading it, I forgot the time. If there wasn't a deadline…'

'I know,' she agreed gently, 'but I'm going to be pretty busy myself for the next few weeks,' she said positively, 'so you will be able to get on with your writing in peace. I'm looking forward to it. It will be all right, Jed, won't it?' she couldn't help asking.

'Yes, Sarah, it will be all right.'

And for a little while, it was. They spent a cosy weekend together in front of the fire, and, although they didn't sleep together, didn't discuss anything that mattered, Jed was more relaxed than he'd been for a long time. He even forgot once or twice to treat her like his sister.

On Monday morning, feeling a little bit nervous, unsure, she rang Mrs McKenzie to make sure it was convenient for the first sitting, and then turned to Jed with a briskness that was belied by the worry in her eyes.

'It will be fine,' he reassured her for the tenth time. 'Are you really sure you want to drive yourself?'

'Yes,' she said positively. 'I have to do it some time. And the roads aren't too bad.'

'No,' he agreed, still watching her. 'But they are wet and a bit slushy.'

'There aren't any bends, or hills... I'll be fine, Jed. I'll ring you when I get there.'

'And come back before it gets dark.'

'Yes. Could I borrow your Polaroid camera, do you think?'

He went to fetch it, and then carried her things down to the car. He waited until she'd reversed out, and watched her drive cautiously away. His green eyes were bleak as he prowled slowly round the house touching things, putting them back, and wished he knew what to do for the best. She *was* getting better, trying so hard, but she looked so fragile still. Perhaps they should discuss it as she wanted, but he truly didn't think she was strong enough yet to thrash it all out—but he knew he was just making excuses to himself.

The phone rang, and he jumped. With a small grimace for the state of his nerves, he hurried to answer it.

Mrs McKenzie opened the door to Sarah herself, smiled warmly and ushered her quickly inside to the fire.

'Coffee first, I think. Mary has it all ready. Mary?' she yelled and there was an answering yell from somewhere beyond the lounge, presumably the kitchen. Two minutes later Mary walked sedately in. She was very large, and not very young. She said something that was entirely incomprehensible to Sarah, set down the tray and retreated.

'A treasure,' Mrs McKenzie said drily. 'She was foisted on me by Fiona.' She began pouring the coffee with a hand that visibly shook and slammed down the coffee-pot in disgust. 'I'm nervous,' she stated. 'Now isn't that silly? Sixty- four years old and I'm nervous. I didn't know what to wear. I must have tried on every dratted outfit I possess.'

'You look very nice—and my hands are shaking more than yours,' Sarah confessed. 'Would you mind very much if I rang Jed to say I'm safely here?'

'Worries, does he? The phone's over there.'

When she'd rung and slowly drunk her coffee, she felt better. 'Do you want it to be a formal pose?'

'Yes. I want to look like a matriarch so that in a hundred years' time someone will look at the painting and say, ''My, but she looks imposing.''' With a definite twinkle in her eyes, she added, 'I keep wondering if I ought to have a stag in the background.'

'I'm not very good with animals,' Sarah warned.

'Oh. Heather? Moorland?'

'Fireplace?'

They grinned at each other, and Sarah went to fetch her camera. Positioning Mrs McKenzie against the dark wood of the fireplace she took several snaps in different positions, and then carefully examined each picture as it cleared. There were two that she liked and she handed them across to her hostess.

'What do you think?'

'That one,' Mrs McKenzie said positively of one and discarded the other.

'Yes, I think so too.'

Repositioning Mrs McKenzie in the appropriate pose, she did several quick pencil sketches for added reference, and smiled. 'I'll start on the painting tomorrow. Block it in and then, let's see, may I come on Wednesday? Maybe for an hour each day after that so you won't get too tired.'

'Sounds fine. Will I see the sketches?' she begged softly.

'Oh, yes, of course.'

Mrs McKenzie examined them for a long time, her face solemn, until Sarah became quite nervous. 'They're only rough working sketches,' she began. 'I mean, don't take that as…'

'Stop babbling,' she ordered. Laying the sketch-book on her knee, she stared at Sarah. 'Why aren't you a professional?' she finally asked.

Startled, Sarah just stared at her.

'I expected—amateur. In fact, I half expected that they wouldn't look like me at all. When Jed first proposed it, I thought it would be a bit of fun. I don't get many visitors, and I thought, oh, well, if it's not very good, we can have a laugh about it and I would donate it to Fiona anyway. But these… Oh, my dear. I think I'm a bit overwhelmed. You've made me look—regal. All that talent,' she continued, 'you could charge a fortune! We never even discussed money—'

'No!' Sarah broke in hurriedly. Thoroughly embarrassed, she denied awkwardly, 'I wasn't going to charge you.'

'You most certainly will!'

'No.'

'Yes, but we'll not discuss it now. Lunch first, and then you're to get off home before it gets dark. Mary!' she yelled.

Driving carefully home, her mind was more on Mrs McKenzie's words than anything else.

She wondered if she ought to refuse to paint her—she really hadn't expected to be paid. And yet, she *wanted* to do the portrait. Already felt committed to doing it. She hadn't felt this eager or motivated since—well, since before she was pregnant.

Pulling into the garage, eager to discuss ev-erything with Jed, she hurried up the steps and inside. Flinging off her coat, sketch-pad and camera clutched to her chest, she started along the hall and met Jed just coming out of the lounge. He was all dressed up, and she stared at him in astonishment.

'How did it go?' he asked with a smile.

'Oh, OK—no, it went really well.' She grinned. 'Why are you…?'

'Show me.' Holding out his hand, he waited for her to put the sketch-book into it. As he flicked over the pages his smile grew. 'Clever girl,' he praised softly. 'You've captured her exactly.'

'Thank you.' Pleased, flattered, she smiled at him, and then frowned. 'Are you just going out?'

'No, we are. You have an hour to get ready.'

'But where are we going?'

'To celebrate my wife's first commission of

the new year, of course. I've booked a table up at the hotel.'

'Oh.'

'Well, don't look so surprised—don't you think you're worth it?'

Still staring at him, her eyes wide, she suddenly gave a slow, delighted smile. 'Yes,' she agreed. 'I do.'

'Then go and get ready.'

Not needing to be told again, she dumped the camera on the hall table and hurried up to her room. See, Sarah? You were wrong, she told herself. He does love you. He wouldn't go to all this trouble if he didn't, would he? No.

Feeling suddenly festive and determined to make the most of their—date, she thought with a little grin of happiness, she got her dark red dress out of the wardrobe and held it against her. It wasn't new, or particularly dressy, but she always felt comfortable in it. She had a shower, carefully made up her face, dressed, and was downstairs five minutes short of the hour he'd stipulated.

Her cheeks were flushed and there was a sparkle in her eyes that had been missing for a long time. Slightly breathless, she stood in front of him. 'Will I do?'

'Oh,' he drawled, a teasing glint in his eyes, 'adequate, I think.'

With a soft laugh, she flung her arms round him and kissed him. Tension shimmered between them, and she felt him stiffen slightly. Forcing herself to lightness, pretending she hadn't noticed, she said brightly, 'And now I've left lipstick all over you.' Taking a clean tissue from her pocket, and with a hand that shook slightly, she wiped it away.

Don't rush things, she cautioned herself. Take it slowly. One step at a time. Don't *overwhelm* him. He didn't like being overwhelmed.

It was only a five-minute drive to the Glentaith Hotel, which was fortunate, because Sarah couldn't think of anything to say. It wasn't that he hadn't wanted her to kiss him, she persuaded herself. She'd taken him by surprise, that was all. Jed needed to *think* about things. Look how he'd been in Bavaria? It had taken him three days to come round after first kissing her.

Yes, that was all it was. Dragging her mind away, trying to pretend that nothing was amiss, that she wasn't worried, she stared at the elegant lines of the hotel that had once been a manor house.

Allowing him to help her out and inside, she halted in shock. She'd expected the inside to complement the outside, but it didn't. Inside was a bewildering array of mirrors that flung their reflections back at them in the most disconcerting fashion.

'Good heavens!' she exclaimed faintly.

'Mmm,' he agreed drily. 'Not for the faint-hearted, is it?'

'No.'

Their outdoor things were taken by a rather solemn young man and she hastily tucked her scarf into her coat pocket before he could disappear.

'Would sir and madam like to have a drink in the bar before dining?'

'Yes, thank you,' Jed agreed with equal solemnity, and she gave a small giggle.

He glanced at her, teasing reproof in his eyes, and she relaxed again.

'Perhaps someone could bring us the menu?' he added quietly.

'Of course.'

'Of course,' he said under his breath. Catching Sarah's hand in his, he led her into the bar. Apart from the barman, who greeted them quietly, it was empty.

'What can I get you?'

Jed glanced at Sarah, and she answered, 'Gin and tonic, please.'

'I'll have the same.' Escorting her to a small table, he sat opposite.

'It's almost like a first date, isn't it?' she asked without thinking. 'Getting to know each other, getting—'

'Did we ever have proper dates?' he interrupted softly.

'No, but we had—fun, didn't we?'

'Yes, we had fun.'

Watching her, examining her face in the soft lighting of the bar, he praised softly, 'You look exceptionally lovely.'

'Do I?' With a little blush, she hastily thanked the barman as he put her drink in front of her, arranged a little dish of peanuts beside her and then returned with Jed's drink.

'You look pretty special too.' But then, he always did.

'What do you want from your life, Sarah?' he asked quietly.

'Want?' A little flicker of panic inside, she looked at him. 'To be happy.'

'Yes.'

'And you?'

'The same. We got a bit off track, didn't we?'

'Yes,' she whispered, then cursed softly under her breath as a waiter halted beside them and handed them the menus.

Opening hers, she made a pretence at reading it, wondering what he was about to say. When he said nothing more, she flicked him a glance to find that he was staring down at his own menu. Heart fluttering, she took a steadying breath. 'Are we on track now, Jed?'

He looked up, held her eyes with his, opened his mouth to answer, and the waiter returned.

'Your table is ready now, sir.'

He could have told him to wait, that *they* weren't ready, but he didn't; he merely closed his menu and nodded.

The waiter took the menus, tucked them under his arm, and led the way into the lobby and across towards the dining room.

All wasn't lost, she told herself. They could talk over dinner, and perhaps, finally, he could tell her what he really wanted. And she could tell him.

'Jed!'

They both halted, turned, and Sarah stared at the most strikingly attractive woman she thought she had ever seen. Tumbled red hair fell to just below her shoulder blades, and bluey-grey eyes dominated a face that was a great deal more than beautiful. Assured, elegant, slightly older than Sarah, the woman stared at Jed, smiled, and then gave a throaty laugh.

'I've just been to your house looking for you!' she exclaimed as she advanced.

'Have you?' he asked quietly. He looked stunned.

CHAPTER FIVE

'HAVE you?' she mimicked. 'Is that the best you can do? It's been over a *year*! Are you dining here? Good, I'll join you.' Her voice was low and husky. Sexy. Flinging off her coat and thrusting it at the waiter, who hastily beckoned someone else to take it, she stood in front of Jed, beamed, and kissed him full on the mouth. Stepping back, she gave another low, throaty laugh. 'Well, don't look so bemused, darling, it's not entirely a coincidence. The London papers picked up the article about you in the local paper, and here I am.' Turning to the waiting waiter, she smiled at him. 'I'm a perfect nuisance, aren't I? But could you set another place?'

'Of course, madam, if you would all like to follow me?'

Feeling numb and unreal, because this beautiful creature could only be Deanna, Sarah slowly turned to look at Jed.

'Sarah, I'm so sorry. I had no idea.'

'No,' she agreed flatly. 'We'd better go in.'

'I can tell her we'd like to dine alone…'

'No, it's all right. Really.' But it wasn't. Of course, it wasn't.

Slowly following Deanna, aware of Jed behind her, she took her place at the table whilst the waiter hastily moved another chair across, summoned someone to lay another place, and handed them back their menus.

Deanna looked at her, looked at Jed, and gave a small apologetic grimace. 'Did I just muscle in? I'm so sorry,' she said to Sarah, 'I didn't realise you were together.'

Forcing a smile, Sarah assured her it was all right.

'Jed and I are old friends,' Deanna said.

'Yes, I know.'

'Sorry,' Jed put in quietly. 'Deanna, this is Sarah. Sarah, Deanna.'

They smiled at each other. Deanna didn't look at all discomfited. Sarah wished she could run away. But she couldn't. She was all grown up now, and, no matter how much it might hurt to see these two together, not by look or deed must she show that it mattered. If she'd been secure in his love, it wouldn't, of course. But she wasn't. She could have wept. Not half an hour ago, she'd been happy, confident that everything was going to be all right.

Had he known Deanna would be here? No, of course not—he'd said so, hadn't he?

'Sarah?'

Hastily glancing up, she stared at her husband, and he smiled at her.

'Are you ready to order?'

'Oh.' Quickly opening her menu, she stared blindly down at it. Fish, she thought. Fish was easy to eat, didn't require much chewing. 'I'll have the salmon.'

'Deanna?' he asked.

'Lord, I don't know!' she exclaimed. 'I'm starving! Are you having a starter, Sarah?'

Sarah shook her head.

'Jed?'

He gave a soft laugh. 'Deanna, you can have anything you want, you don't have to see what everyone else is having.'

'I know, but if I'm having a starter and no one else is…'

'Then we'll all have a starter. Sarah, do you think you could manage some soup?'

'Yes, of course.'

When they'd ordered and the waiter had departed, Jed asked in some amusement, an amusement that to Sarah seemed slightly false, 'How was the adventure?' Turning to Sarah, he explained, 'The last time I saw Deanna, she was heading off up the Amazon.'

'Oh, sounds exciting.'

'Well, it wasn't!' Deanna grinned. 'Because I didn't go. I went to the South of France instead. Much more civilised.' Sending Jed a teasing glance, she asked, 'Jealous?'

'Not in the least.'

'Liar,' she scoffed amiably. 'You love France.'

'I love a lot of places.'

She laughed. 'Yes, and now that you're rich and famous I expect you visit them all.' Glancing at Sarah, she asked, 'Do you go with him? I used to go to places with him sometimes. I hope he's nice to you; he wasn't always nice to me. Ah, food!' she exclaimed thankfully. 'And where is everyone? This place is like the *Mary Celeste*.'

'It's February,' Jed said drily. '*Everywhere* is dead in February.'

'But they must have some guests in this hotel!' Glancing disparagingly round, she stared at the only other occupant of the dining room, a rather elderly lady who was sitting across on the other side. Thanking the waiter with a charm that seemed to come naturally to her, she began on her soup, and both Sarah and

Jed did the same. Sarah managed half of hers,
then sat staring out at the softly falling snow
beyond the wide windows. She wondered why
the curtains hadn't been drawn. Perhaps someone had forgotten.

Jed was laughing softly at something
Deanna had said and Sarah dragged her attention back, pinning a smile on her face as she
tried to look interested. They both tried to include her in the conversation, but they spoke
about people she didn't know and could there-
fore have no interest in.

They looked so right together, she thought
miserably. Both attractive, both worldly.
Whatever had he seen in herself?

The meal seemed interminable. Jed probably thought she was sulking, but she wasn't,
she just didn't know what to say to this glam-
orous creature who seemed to have been round
the world several times; knew people Sarah
had only ever read about. And Jed knew them
too. It put her own small adventures to shame,
didn't it? And she'd thought herself so—cos-
mopolitan. Her friends in Bavaria had laughed
at some of her adventures, but they rather
paled in comparison to Deanna's.

'Have you ever been there, Sarah?'

Glancing up, she gave an apologetic smile. 'Sorry, wool-gathering. Have I been where?'

'Moscow.'

'No.'

'You must go. Get Jed to take you. It's the most amazing place.'

'Yes, so I've heard.' And Deanna was trying very hard to include her, make her feel at ease. Deanna wasn't hateful, or spiteful, a bit shallow maybe, but not an unkind person. It might have been easier if she had been. And Deanna and Jed obviously had so much in common. If it hadn't been for the baby, would he now be back with Deanna? Living the sort of life he'd always lived, the sort of life he liked?

'And now you're painting Mrs McKenzie,' Deanna continued amiably. 'How do you get on with her?'

'Fine. She seems very nice.'

'She is,' she laughed. 'But I don't think she ever approved of me. I'm a bit...'

'Flighty?' Jed put in drily.

She grimaced. 'Perhaps. I get bored easily,' she explained to Sarah. 'But Jed and I usually end up in each other's pockets. Don't we?' she asked him almost flirtatiously, and then laughed. 'Don't take any notice of me, Sarah,

Jed and I know each other too well to pretend that neither of us have other interests, other—loves. And perhaps you could paint *me*. I've always rather fancied a portrait to hang over the fireplace.'

'You'd never sit still long enough,' Jed disparaged. 'Anyway, you don't have a fireplace.'

'Yes, I do,' she contradicted. 'Uncle Lionel left me his house in London.'

'Lucky you.'

'Mmm.' She suddenly gave an enormous yawn. 'Sorry, but I'm *so* tired. I'm not used to such a long drive, and tomorrow I'm heading further north to stay with some friends.' Her smile for Jed alone, she added softly, 'I'll only be gone a few days—will you still be here when I get back?'

'I imagine so.'

'Can we meet up?' she pleaded. 'Catch up on old times? You won't mind, will you, Sarah?'

'No, of course not.' What else could she say?

'Good. I knew you looked sensible.' Quickly finishing her coffee, she added, 'And now I'm going to leave you in peace.' Leaning across the table, she kissed Jed on the mouth and got to her feet. He courteously rose, and with a last smile she walked away. She left a long silence behind her.

Staring at Jed as he watched Deanna depart, Sarah felt a slow anger begin to burn. Leave them in peace? Now that she'd successfully ruined their evening? No, not *their* evening. Hers. Jed hadn't minded her presence at all, had he? 'Does she usually assume that she can steal you away from whatever love you happen to be with?' she asked waspishly.

He looked surprised, then shook his head. 'No,' he denied. 'It's just her way. Deanna doesn't always think before she speaks.'

Unlike Jed, who always seemed to think very carefully. 'But then, she didn't know I was your wife, did she?' she continued. 'Not that I'm not glad to have met her,' she added tersely. 'The imagination is always worse than the reality, isn't it? You'll have a lot to talk about, a lot to catch up on. Shall we go?'

'Sarah…'

'And how nice that I'm sensible,' she added pithily. 'I'll wait for you in the lobby.' Getting to her feet, she walked out. Collecting their coats, she stood fuming by a mirrored pillar.

He joined her five minutes later. 'I didn't tell her we were married,' he reproved quietly as he took his coat from her, 'because I thought it was something I should tell her in private.'

'Why? Because she's in love with you?' she asked stiffly. 'Although it seems a funny sort of love to me if she doesn't mind you having other lovers. Or does she tend to make scenes? Is that it?'

'No, it's because we're old friends and I didn't want her to be embarrassed in front of you.'

But he didn't mind her feeling awkward in front of Deanna, did he? Or hadn't he even noticed that she'd felt like a spare part?

'Shall we go?' he asked quietly and in the sort of voice that presaged a row.

Well, good, a row was just what she felt like.

'And whatever it is you're thinking or feeling,' he continued, 'Deanna is just an old friend. I'm sorry the celebration turned into a threesome...'

'But it wasn't your fault. Was it?' Head high, she led the way out.

Deanna had been sparkling and witty, and she'd sat there like a lump. He must be comparing them, mustn't he? How could he help it? Feeling all trembly inside, threatened, angry, hurt, she waited for him to unlock the car and then climbed inside. Jed was married to her. Was in love with her, supposedly. But when had he ever said so voluntarily without her saying it first?

Stop it, Sarah told herself fiercely as he climbed in beside her. Deanna wasn't a threat. She wouldn't allow her to be, which meant she should shut up about it, but she couldn't leave it alone. 'When will you tell her?'

'Tell her?' he asked, his voice as stiff as hers.

'That we're married.'

'When she comes back.'

And then they could talk, all by themselves, without Sarah to hear what they were saying. How long would she stay? she wondered bleakly. Long enough to get to know Jed again? Make him her own once more?

Had the sight of her rekindled old feelings? Made him realise what he'd done? And the silence in the car was unbearable. 'Why was she going up the Amazon?' she asked in a voice that sounded brittle.

'Mmm? Oh, a whim. Deanna is full of whims.' He spoke indifferently, as though it didn't much matter, but she suspected that it did.

'What does she do?'

'Do?' he asked vaguely.

'Yes, or does she have private means?' she persisted. 'Going up the Amazon, or even the South of France, isn't cheap.'

'No.'

So what did she *do*? She wanted to yell at him. Feeling lost and helpless, not knowing whether to pursue it or ignore it, she stared out at the falling snow. She'd always wanted to be tall, like Deanna. She didn't think she had ever wanted red hair, but... And was he regretting that he had ever married? Regretting ever having met her?

When he pulled into the garage, she got quickly out without waiting for him to help her. It felt very cold. Shoving her hands into her pockets, she waited for him to close the garage doors, then preceded him up the steep steps. She heard him slip, curse and she whirled round.

'What have you done?'

'Nothing.'

'Jed!'

'It's nothing, go on, we'll freeze to death out here.' He sounded irritable.

Hurrying up the last few steps, she waited

for him to open the door, then turned to stare at him in the hall. 'Did you bang your leg?'

'No, it's all right.'

'It is not all right!' Finding renewed focus for her fear, her frustration, she snapped, 'It is allowed to complain, you know! Ever since it happened you limp bravely round making me feel... I just wish you'd stop being so—stoical! If it hurts, bloody say so! Why can't you be like everybody else and shout about it? Curse, swear.... It's not normal to be so...'

'Stoical,' he repeated quietly. 'All right, it hurts. Happy?'

'No.' Turning her back, she flung off her coat. 'Do you want her?' she demanded. 'Deanna?'

'No.'

'She wants you!'

'No, Sarah she doesn't.' Brushing past her, he limped into the lounge.

Following him, she stared at his rigid back as he bent to stir the fire into life. 'Did you just realise what you were missing?' she demanded.

'No.'

'Everyone expected you would marry her.'

'Then everyone was wrong, weren't they?

Go to bed, Sarah. This is a conversation that's going nowhere.'

'The reason for our marriage no longer exists…'

'I'm aware of that.' Dear God, how he was aware of it.

He heard her leave, listened to her footsteps as she hurried up the stairs, and then the muffled bang of her bedroom door. With a deep sigh, he shoved the poker back on its rack and sat to rub his knee. Eyes bleak, he stared at the fire. Deanna, Deanna, he thought tiredly, you choose the worst moments to re-enter my life. And yet, maybe it was for the best; perhaps it was time he and Sarah both took their heads out of the sand. They had to resolve it, didn't they? And soon.

Getting awkwardly to his feet, wincing at the pain that shot through his leg, he limped slowly upstairs to Sarah's room. She was standing in the middle of the floor, her back to him, and she stiffened when she heard him enter.

'Sarah?' When she didn't answer, he walked up behind her and put his hands on her shoulders. 'I'm sorry,' he apologised. 'It was supposed to be a nice, quiet little dinner party, just the two of us. Deanna took me by surprise, and, yes, my legs hurts, and my head, and I didn't handle it very well, did I?'

Slumping slightly, she sighed, 'No, I'm the one who's sorry. I had no right to behave like that. She made me feel inadequate, I think, reminded me of how I used to be.' Somehow needing to prove the wound, she asked, 'Did you really never want to marry her?'

'No,' he said simply. Gently turning her, he stared down into her wan face. 'She was good company, fun to be with…'

Good in bed? She wanted to ask.

'But she has a low boredom threshold. Full of nervous energy, she always wanted to be doing something. I was working, and often away, and so, if I couldn't do it, or didn't want to, she would find someone else who would.'

'She doesn't work?'

'No—at least, not very often. She does some modelling, TV advertisements, but mostly she expects other people to fund her.'

'But that's immoral!' she exclaimed.

'Not to Deanna. All her life she's been spoilt. I don't think she even realises how she expects it, *needs* it even. She's exhausting, yet interesting,' he added fairly. 'A bit like a cosmic force, I suppose. Moody one minute, full of laughter the next. We would see each other when we were both in the same vicinity, or she would suddenly fly out to see me wherever I was working. Something would annoy her or distract her and she would disappear again, sometimes for months on end. And then, as though nothing had happened, back she would come and expect everything to be the same.'

'A social butterfly?'

'Yes.'

'But you are fond of her.'

'Yes, I am fond of her.'

'As she is of you.'

'Yes.'

Trying to lighten the moment, trying, without the words, to unsay all she had said downstairs, she murmured, 'Your air of brooding intensity, I expect.'

'Brooding?' he asked in surprise.

'Yes. It's very attractive. The dark and brooding stranger who hides a chequered past. There is sometimes an air of mystery about you, as though you could be dangerous.'

'And that's *attractive*?' he asked in astonishment.

'Yes,' she agreed simply. 'To women.'

'To you?'

'Of course to me.' Unable to leave it, even though she knew she should, unable to dismiss it, she continued, 'And when she comes back, how long will she stay?'

'I don't know. Not long, I expect,' he reassured her gently. Reaching out, he touched one finger to the corner of her mouth. 'Don't worry about it, Sarah. All I want is for you to get well.'

So that he could leave her with a clear conscience? 'That's all I want, too,' she murmured.

He smiled, but it was a tense smile, forced. Why? Because she'd denigrated his precious Deanna? Because the other woman was more to him than he'd said? And he wouldn't ever hurt his wife by leaving her until she was well, would he?

'All right now?' he asked gently.

'Yes.' What else could she say.

'Then go to bed. Goodnight, Sarah.' Dropping a kiss on her hair, he left.

Sinking down on the edge of the bed, she stared at nothing. Had he got fed up with Deanna's capricious ways? Put her out of his mind in that strong-willed way of his and got on with his life? It didn't mean he didn't still love her though, did it? There had been something between them; tension, challenge, flirtation. Sarah had never kept in touch with old

boyfriends and so she didn't know if that was
how ex-lovers behaved. She couldn't imagine
it herself. And when Deanna came back, was
he going to tell her that, although he was married *now*, as soon as Sarah was well he would
be free again?

In the midst of despair and misery, she
slowly got ready for bed. The evening had
started out with such high hopes, too.

The next day, with Jed working in his study,
Sarah set up her easel in the bedroom, because
it had the best light, and began on her painting.
With the small Polaroid pinned to the apex of
the wooden frame, her sketches propped up on
the dressing table, she began. At first, her mind
was more on Deanna and Jed than her painting, as it had been all night, but slowly, as she
became more and more absorbed, her fears began to fade into the background. She'd been
foolish, she assured herself. Overreacting. She
should have been nicer to Deanna, shown Jed
she really was a mature adult.

The blue was too harsh, she decided, her
head on one side. It needed to be softer.
Changing it, lightening it until she was satis-
fied, she became more and more engrossed.
With her tongue peeping out from the corner

of her mouth, she jumped like a startled hare when there was a little tap at the door.

'Come in.'

Mrs Reeves put her head inside, then beamed when she saw that Sarah wasn't angry at being disturbed.

'Jed said you were busy and not to bother you if you didn't answer my knock, but I thought you'd be wanting some lunch. I left Jed some sandwiches and coffee and brought up the same for you.'

Sarah smiled. 'Thank you, Mrs Reeves. Could you put them on the dressing table for me?'

She walked across to do so, and then stood looking at the sketches of Mrs McKenzie. 'Well!' she exclaimed. 'I'll not need to be asking who it is, will I?'

Assuming it was a compliment, Sarah grinned.

Still looking at the sketches, Mrs Reeves continued, 'I can't tell you how glad we all are that you're feeling better.'

'Thank you,' Sarah said awkwardly. 'I'm sorry I've been so, well, you must have thought poor Jed to have such a…'

'We thought no such thing!' she denied fiercely. 'Anyone with eyes to see could tell you were poorly. But you're getting better, putting on weight...'

'Thanks to your excellent meals... I saw Deanna last night,' she added as casually as she could, and waited, breath almost held, for a response.

'Aye.' Mrs Reeves sighed heavily. 'I heard she was back. Came here, did she?'

'Yes, no, I mean, we saw her at the hotel. You obviously knew her.'

'Yes,' she agreed. 'Summer and winter, that one. Never knew which she was going to be. Frosty or flowery. She'll burn herself out one of these days—can't live your life either up or down, can you?'

'No,' Sarah agreed inadequately.

'She won't stay long, she never does. Don't you go worrying about her, Sarah.'

'No, and thank you for being so kind about everything, especially as I've been such a—weed.'

'Nonsense,' she denied briskly. 'We didn't know how to help you, you see. Didn't know what was best. You seemed so grieved. What was it, then?' she asked gently. 'Did someone die in the accident?'

Feeling her eyes fill with tears, she took a

deep breath to contain them and said quickly, 'Yes, someone died. And it—hurt.'

'Oh, sweetheart!' Mrs Reeves exclaimed softly and with such compassion that Sarah's tears overflowed. Folding Sarah against her, Mrs Reeves gave her the comfort she so sorely needed. 'Poor wee girl. We never knew all the details, we didn't know someone had died, so obviously dear to you both. And you had no mother to comfort you, did you? Jed said you were brought up by your granny.'

'Yes.' Sniffing hard, she allowed herself to rest for a moment against the housekeeper's shoulder, and then she straightened determinedly, took a tissue from the box on the dressing table, blew her nose hard, and forced a smile.

'I'll not tell anyone if you don't want it known,' she promised. 'Now, you sit down and eat those sandwiches,' she ordered briskly, 'and drink your coffee whilst it's hot. If you need me, need someone to talk to, you know where I am, don't you?'

'Yes.' Reaching out, Sarah squeezed Mrs Reeves' hand. 'Thank you.'

'Nothing to thank me for,' she said. 'Jed's taking it hard, too, isn't he? Not that he'd ever say. Like his mother in that respect, keeps things to himself. Not always good to bottle things up.'

'No. You knew her?' she asked carefully. 'Jed's mother?'

'Yes. They lived here for a while.'

'He said she was stoic.'

'Aye,' she agreed softly as though she was looking back, remembering. 'Hard for a woman on her own.'

'She was a widow?' she asked in surprise. Jed had never said. But then, he never mentioned his background at all.

'Widow?' she echoed. 'Aye, maybe. Don't work too long without a break,' she instructed briskly. 'Get out in the fresh air.' Peering from the window as though to make sure the air was still fresh, she nodded. 'More snow on the way,' she prophesied again and walked quietly out.

Sarah sat slowly eating her sandwiches, and wondered what Mrs Reeves had been carefully not saying about Jed's mother. That she hadn't been a widow? She could have pressed it, she supposed, but maybe it would be best to ask Jed. And maybe it would have been better to have told Mrs Reeves that it was their unborn baby who had died, not an adult as she clearly had assumed, but Sarah wasn't sure she was ready for that yet. And maybe Mrs Reeves saw Jed's troubles more clearly than she did. Sarah was maybe too close to it all to view anything objectively.

Finishing her lunch, she decided she would take Mrs Reeves' advice and go for a walk and clear her head before doing some more on the painting. Carrying the tray down to the kitchen, she put on her boots and coat. She searched for her scarf in the pocket to put on, but found it missing. She cursed realising it must have fallen out up at the hotel. Dragging on her woolly hat and gloves, she took a deep breath, determinedly, and tapped on the study door before putting her head inside. Jed was leaning back in his chair, feet on the open bottom drawer of the desk, a pencil between his teeth, and staring at his laptop that was open on the blotter. His hair needed cutting again, she saw, and she wanted to touch it, run her fingers through it. Feeling sad and unsure, she walked silently up behind him and dropped a kiss on his hair.

Startled, he turned his head to look up at her. 'Hello,' he greeted. 'Finished for the day?'

'No, I'm going out to get some fresh air.

Why don't you come with me?' she asked impulsively.

He stared at her, green eyes thoughtful, then thumped his feet to the floor. 'Yes, why not?' Removing the pencil and tossing it onto the desk, he pressed a button to save what he'd already written on the computer and got to his feet. Pressing a kiss to her cheek, he walked out and into the hall.

Relieved, grateful, she watched him tug on his own boots and unhook his sheepskin. 'Come along, then, Mrs Dane, let's go mess up some virgin snow.'

'Yes. Jed, I'm sorry about last night,' she blurted.

'Shh, it's all right. Come on.' Taking her hand, he pulled her out the front door and helped her down the front steps.

Was it all right? Really? She didn't know, but she had to believe it, didn't she? Taking a deep breath of the cold, crisp air, she stared up at the sky. It was a clear, bright blue. Why Mrs Reeves thought there would be more snow, she had no idea; there wasn't a snow cloud to be seen.

Instead of taking the road, Jed tugged her onto the moor, or the glen, or whatever it was called, and she looked back at their footprints in the snow. It was only a few inches deep as yet, although up on the hills—mountains, she corrected herself—it looked a lot deeper. Jed was still favouring his left leg, although not as much as he had been, and she opened her mouth to ask if he was all right walking on uneven ground, then closed it again. Last night's mention of it hadn't been received very well, had it? And he wasn't a child. He knew better than she what he was capable of.

Unaware that Mrs Reeves watched them go, a small frown on her face, they climbed slowly to a mound of jumbled rocks and then turned to survey the scene below them. Everywhere was white and beautiful. There was no wind to chill them, and, with the watery sun shining on the loch, everywhere looked peaceful and clean. Looking to the left, to the row of houses where smoke curled lazily from most of the chimneys, she said quietly, 'Mrs Reeves asked if someone had died in the accident. I said yes, but didn't say—who.' Because it was a who, at three and a half months, it had been their little baby. 'She won't tell anyone else unless we want her to.'

He squeezed her hand.

'She said she remembered your mother.'

'Yes, I imagine she did.'

'There were just the two of you?'

'Yes.'

'She was a widow?'

'No,' he denied quietly. He glanced at her, and then added, 'I have no idea who my father was. She would never say.'

'She wasn't married?'

'No.'

'Poor lady. It must have been very hard back then.'

'Yes.'

'Tell me,' she pleaded.

He gave a small sigh, stared out over the landscape. 'I don't know why she kept me, why she didn't have me adopted…'

'Because she loved you, I expect,' Sarah murmured, she supposed, in comfort.

'No,' he denied. 'Or, if she did,' he qualified somewhat drily, 'it was never something she shared with me, but she had a terrific sense of duty. Something of a martyr to the cause, was my mother. There was never much money, but I was fed, clothed, educated. She made no secret of the fact that she was an unmarried mother. I sometimes wonder if she even took a pride in it.'

'And so everyone at school knew you were…'

'A bastard? Yes.'

'And it made you stoical.'

He laughed. 'Yes.'

And a loner. Was that why he had married her? So that her baby *would* have a father? It wasn't something she was going to ask. Not now, at any rate. 'And when you grew up, you bought the house you'd lived in?' she murmured.

'Mmm. I'm not entirely sure why. I passed it one day. It was for sale, and so I bought it. I sometimes do things on impulse.'

Like marrying her? Turning her attention to the scenery, she sighed. 'It's beautiful here, isn't it? Not unlike Bavaria, in a way. Different architecture, different people, but not totally unlike. I'm getting better, Jed.'

'I know.' He glanced at her and gave a faint, sad smile at the ridiculous hat that covered her ears and eyebrows. 'You have a delightful nose, Mrs Dane.'

Turning, she smiled at him. 'And you have a delightful everything.'

'Do I?' he asked quietly as he searched her small face. And then his mood changed again. 'Come on, before we both get a chill. I'm not as fast as I used to be, and going downhill is a great deal harder than going up.'

'I'll help you,' she promised with a forced grin. 'Lean on me.'

'If I lean on you we'll both end up on our backs.'

'Sounds good,' she teased, and he laughed. But that sounded forced too.

'Come on. I've got a chapter to finish, and you've got a painting to do.'

With a little *moue* of disappointment, a pretence that she didn't mind his avoidance of intimacy, which she did, desperately, she spread her arms wide and began to run downhill. Reaching the road, she stopped to wait for him. Cheeks glowing, nose red, an ache in her heart that seemed as if it would never go away, she deliberately didn't watch him follow her. He wouldn't want her to see him stumble. She didn't know how she knew that, she just did.

There wasn't a ripple to be seen on the loch, not the wake of a fish, nor the movement of a weed. It was as smooth as glass. 'Has it ever iced over?' she asked as she heard him come up behind her.

'I believe so, and if it does again this year I don't want you walking on it.'

Turning her head, she smiled up at him. 'I won't,' she promised. 'You have a nice,

healthy glow. See how good I am for you?'
And then remembered that she hadn't been
good for him at all. Or, not lately. 'I meant,'
she blurted. 'I mean…'

He put his arms round her and held her back
against his chest. 'Shh. No harking back. We
only look forward, remember?'

'Yes,' she whispered. The doctor had said
that, and Jed seemed to have taken it as gos-
pel.

'Come on. We have work to do.' With a
last hug, he released her, took her hand and
pulled her along towards the steps.

Cursing her stupidity because it had
changed the happy mood, she wondered how
long it would be before she *did* stop looking
back.

'If everyone thought before they spoke,
Sarah,' he said gently, 'there would be no conversation. Stop minding my feelings, or even
assuming you know what they are, or what
I'm thinking. Now, go and get on with this
magnificent portrait.'

Turning to him, she said quietly, 'It *is* going
to be magnificent. I can feel it.'

'You think I don't know that? You're a very
talented lady.'

With a last smile, she pressed a kiss to his

chin and went upstairs. Soon he would come
to her, she promised herself. Soon he would
share her bed again. And Deanna couldn't be
that important, could she? He'd said himself
that she was moody. But then, she herself had
been pretty moody lately.

Wednesday and Thursday were the same.
She arrived at Mrs McKenzie's, had coffee
with her, painted for an hour, and then they
had lunch. She made sure she was home before it got dark. Friday was different. She arrived as usual, they had their coffee and then
Mary walked in and announced loudly. 'It's
Friday.'

'I know it's Friday, Mary,' Mrs McKenzie
said crossly and in some perplexity.

'The second Friday in the month.'

She stared at Mary, and Mary stared back.
'Well, why on earth didn't you remind me?'

'I am reminding you.'

Looking from one to the other, Sarah asked,
'Is there a problem?'

'Yes. Sarah, I'm sorry,' she apologised. 'On
the second Friday in the month I have some
friends over to play bridge. Oh, goodness, that
sounds like them now. I'll tell them to go...'

'Don't be silly, one day isn't going to make
any difference.'

'But what about your lunch?'

'I'll have it at home. I'm quite capable of making myself a sandwich, you know.'

Still looking worried, Mrs McKenzie asked Mary to show her guests into the back room.

'Don't worry about it,' Sarah insisted as she began to pack up her things. 'I'll come tomorrow.'

'I really am sorry...'

'It doesn't matter, truly.'

Accompanied by Mrs McKenzie, Sarah walked into the hall to get her outdoor things.

'Where's your hat and scarf?' she scolded. 'Look at you, it's cold out there.'

'I'll be in the car.' She smiled. 'Don't fuss.' Kissing Mrs McKenzie goodbye, she left, but her hostess's mention of a scarf reminded her. As she was early for once, she might as well go up to the hotel and see if they could find it.

Parking on the forecourt, she hurried inside out of the wind. Trying to avoid her many reflections in the mirrors, she walked across to the desk. The receptionist had her head down and was writing something in a book.

'Excuse me,' Sarah began.

The girl looked up, gave an automatic smile.

'I believe I left my scarf here the other night…'

'Blue silk?' she interrupted.

'Yes,' Sarah agreed gratefully.

Groping under the desk, the woman produced it, handed it across, and went back to the ledger.

With a small smile, a little shake of her head, Sarah turned to go and met herself in yet another mirror. Chuckling, she started to move off, and then stopped, because also reflected in the mirror were the images of Jed, and Deanna.

CHAPTER SIX

ROOTED to the spot, Sarah continued to stare at their reflections. They were in a room somewhere behind her, close together. Deanna's palms were flat against Jed's chest and his hands encircled her wrists. Trying to move her away? Or draw her closer? And then the images were blocked out by an elderly gentleman walking across the lobby behind her. When he'd passed, the images were closer. Mouth to mouth.

With an inarticulate little cry, she hurried out to the car. Switching on the engine, she reversed out. They were saying goodbye, that was all it was. All perfectly innocent. They hadn't been hiding; they'd been in plain view of anyone passing. Can we meet up when I get back? Deanna had said, and now, obviously, they were. Had he now told her he was married? Was he consoling her, explaining… And he must have walked up, mustn't he? Unless Deanna had collected him. It was a long walk for someone with a bad leg. But if

you desperately wanted to see someone, a bad
leg wouldn't stop you, would it?

So busy wondering, speculating, fighting
down demons of jealousy, she had no memory
of the drive home. She was stupid, she scolded
herself; she could have driven off the road.
She'd been wrapped up in her own little world
since the accident, she hadn't paid attention to
anything. If Jed was seeking a happier com-
panion, it didn't necessarily mean he wanted
Deanna back. And when he got home, he
would tell her he'd seen Deanna, they would
laugh about it and everything would be all
right. Laugh? They hadn't laughed in a long
time. Hadn't talked properly in a long time.
Hadn't slept together, hadn't kissed, but she'd
kept reassuring herself that everything was all
right, and yet it still wasn't. Of course it
wasn't. He was being kind, avuncular because
he was fond of her, and wouldn't want to hurt
her, but if he'd loved…

Shutting her eyes tight, she leaned her head
back on the seat. She'd accused him of not
wanting to talk about it, but she hadn't either,
had she? She'd only wanted reassurance that
he still loved her—if he ever had.

Everyone had been surprised, hadn't they,
that he was married? Everyone had hinted at

his love of freedom. Domesticity wasn't for Jed... Jed with babies... She'd stifled him... Not deliberately, not on purpose, but if it hadn't been for the baby he would still be free, wouldn't he?

Feeling depressed and frightened, she switched off the ignition and then just sat for a while, thinking. Did she love him enough to let him go? Did she love him enough to pretend she no longer loved him? Because it would have to be that way, wouldn't it? He wouldn't just take his freedom on her say-so, would he? He was much too honourable for that, and he probably knew how much she loved him, how much she relied on him, at the moment, anyway. Things couldn't go back to how they had been, and so it might be best if she went away. But did he *want* his freedom? Remembering him how he had been, and how he was now, she bit her lip, forced back the tears. How could she bear to leave him? How could she?

She didn't know how long she sat there getting colder and colder—minutes, hours. But she finally roused herself and went indoors. Think about it, Sarah, she told herself. Think about it rationally. There were so many signs

that he no longer loved her. Signs she had dismissed, pretended not to see.

Taking off her coat, she walked into the
lounge. Removing the fire-guard, she held her
hands out to the glowing embers. She was no
longer hungry, instead there was a hard lump
in her chest. She made up the fire so that it
blazed, and curled up in the chair. She loved
him, but what sort of life would it be if she
held onto him out of pity? Could she bear to
see him day after day grow more and more
unhappy?

The front door closed with a quiet click, and
she jumped.

'Sarah?'

'In here,' she called thickly.

She heard him limp along the hall, heard the
door open behind her.

'You're home early.'

'Yes,' she agreed. 'Mrs McKenzie had her
bridge friends over.' Taking a small breath,
she turned to face him. 'Been for your walk?'

'Yes.'

'How far did you get today?'

He didn't immediately answer, just walked
to stand opposite her. Face concerned, he
asked gently, 'What's wrong?'

'Nothing. So, how far did you get?' She

sounded anxious, brittle, and she mustn't. 'I've been thinking… This isn't working, Jed, is it?' She hurried on. 'I can't keep on pretending…and when I saw you…'

'Saw me?' he asked with careful neutrality.

'Yes. I went up to the hotel to get my scarf that I left there the other night…'

'And saw me with Deanna?'

'Yes. You were kissing her.'

'Yes.'

Looking away, she stared once more at the fire. 'None of my business, of course, because, well, because…' Just say it, Sarah! Just say you no longer love him! But she couldn't. 'Did you tell her we were married?'

'Yes.'

'But not for much longer?'

He said nothing and she turned to look at him again; her eyes anxious, face set, she waited.

'If I make you feel so insecure,' he said with a sort of flat deliverance that scraped her nerves raw, 'then it's obvious I'm not the right man for you.'

'No,' she whispered, her voice barely audible. 'And if I hadn't been pregnant, you would never have married me, would you?'

'No,' he agreed. 'Any more than you would have married me.'

Opening her mouth to dispute it, she changed her mind. 'I did try…' she began, but her throat filled with tears.

'I know.'

He looked tired and sad, and she supposed he was. The ending of a marriage was always sad. And it was the end, she knew that. Had known it for weeks really, just wouldn't admit it to herself. Vision blurred, she turned her face away.

'Have you eaten?'

She shook her head.

'I'll get you a sandwich…'

'No, I'm not really hungry. I'll go for a walk, I think, get some fresh air.' Getting to her feet, limbs heavy, she walked to the door, then halted. Her back to him, she whispered thickly, 'I did love you, Jed.' Do. Still do. So much.

'Yes.'

Yes, and so it would be best if she left quietly. No fuss, no bother, just leave. Tears freezing on her cheeks, she walked down to the loch. Did the bus still run to Glasgow? The bus that Jed used to catch as a boy? Where did it go from? The village? She could ask.

Go there now, and ask. She could get a train from Glasgow, use her much abused credit card. If she could borrow the bus fare... She would need to get a job, of course... Biting her lip, trying not to think about him, she began to walk along the road. Snow crunched under her boots, and the wind found every opening in her clothing, explored her body with chilled fingers.

She wouldn't tell him she was leaving—not that he would be expecting her to stay, she supposed, not after what they'd said... She would leave a note, perhaps. She could go to Mrs McKenzie's in the morning, collect the painting to finish later, when she was settled, and if there wasn't a bus tomorrow, well, she would take the car. Jed would have to retrieve it. Perhaps Fiona would run him in. Or Deanna. But could she leave without him seeing her? She wouldn't be able to bear saying goodbye.

She would think of something. Smuggle her rucksack down to the car tonight perhaps.

Her decision made, with an empty place where her heart should be, she pushed into the newsagent's to make enquiries. The bus left at ten, she was told, and so now she must go back to the house, make her peace with Jed.

She didn't want to leave on a row, or argument, and she certainly didn't want him to ever feel guilty.

He was in the kitchen when she returned, cooking and she gave a small, sad, smile, watched him with hungry eyes. 'That smells nice,' she commented, and he turned, obviously startled. She rushed on, 'I'm sorry about earlier, for what I said. I was just feeling...'

'Lost?'

'Yes,' she agreed gratefully. 'How long will dinner be?'

'About an hour.'

She nodded. 'Then I'll go and have a nice soak in the bath.' She wanted desperately to touch him, hold him one last time, but then he would know how she felt. Eyes prickling with tears, she turned quickly away, and went upstairs.

You mustn't cry any more, Sarah. No more. You have to start a new life, be brave, strong, the way you used to be.

After dinner, they sat in the lounge for a while watching television, or pretending to. Mostly she just watched Jed, storing up memories... What was he thinking? she wondered. Feeling? It hurt so much... 'I think I'll go to bed,' she said quickly. 'Goodnight, Jed.'

'Goodnight. Oh, and Sarah?' he called after her. His voice sounded as husky as hers. 'Duncan asked if I'd go with him in the morning to look at a car. Would you mind?'

'No, of course not,' she said quickly, too quickly, because it was all working out, wasn't it? 'I might even go to Mrs McKenzie's, do some more on her portrait. I also need to go into the village—could you lend me some money?' she added hesitantly.

He looked hurt for a moment. 'Not lend, no. Give.' Taking some money from his pocket, he handed it to her. 'I should be back about lunchtime, and then we'll talk,' he promised, his eyes bleak. 'A proper talk. Get everything settled.'

'Yes,' she agreed.

Settled? she wondered, as she walked upstairs. As in divorce? As in financial arrangements? No, she wanted none of that. He had given her all he had to give, more than she'd ever been entitled to, and she wouldn't take anything more from him.

With Jed out of the way, she could take her suitcase, couldn't she? Pack everything up. Not now, but in the morning, after he'd gone. Now, she would write her note.

Sitting at the dressing table, she began,

'Dear Jed,' and then just stared at the paper in despair. What could she say? I love you too much to try and keep you? I love you enough to let you go? Chewing the end of her pen, she finally began to write. She tried to make it ambiguous, not actually say she didn't love him because lying seemed somehow a cheat. She knew she rambled; half-finished sentences, explanations, and it probably made no sense at all, but she felt she couldn't go without saying *something*. Tears flowed too freely, damp blotches splattering the three pages she eventually covered. She didn't bother to read it through, just ended it simply with, 'Be happy.'

Her hands shook as she folded it, put it into an envelope and wrote his name on the front. Then she got ready for bed. She didn't sleep very much, and when she got up in the morning her eyes were puffy from her tears. Cold water repaired some of the damage, but it wouldn't take a genius to see how she had spent the night.

Jed didn't comment on her appearance, however. He merely gave her one long, sombre glance before dishing up her breakfast. She managed to eat most of it, trying to seem as normal as possible. Jed, too, seemed to be making an effort. There was a soft tap on the front door, and she stared at him, eyes wide. Almost time.

'That will be Duncan,' he said quietly.

'Yes.'

'Will you be all right?'

'Yes,' she managed. 'Go.' Dear God, go quickly.

He nodded, looking as though he might say something, and then quietly left.

Her throat felt blocked. She wasn't sure she could go through with this, but, taking a deep breath, she hurried into the front room to watch him go. Her last sight of him. He turned at the bottom of the steps to look back at the house, as if he knew, and then he climbed into Duncan's Land Rover and was gone. 'I love you,' she whispered through her tears. Feeling a sob rise, she hastily swallowed it and returned to the kitchen.

She cleared up, left everything tidy, put the guard in front of the lounge fire, and then went upstairs to pack. When she was ready, her eyes were red and puffy again from fresh tears, and her nose was blocked. She propped the letter for him on her dressing table, picked up her suitcase, and left.

She drove slowly and carefully to Mrs

McKenzie's house, afraid that even at this late stage something would happen to prevent her leaving—a flat tyre, a skid—but nothing happened, and she parked where she normally parked.

Walking up the path, she took a deep breath, and knocked.

'Sorry to come unannounced,' she apologised quickly as Mary let her in. 'I'll only be two minutes. Is Mrs McKenzie…?'

'In the lounge.'

'Thank you.'

With a quick smile, a ghastly parody of her usual one, she hurried into the front room.

'Sarah?' Mrs McKenzie exclaimed in surprise. 'I wasn't expecting you today. Are you all right?' she asked in concern. 'You look…'

'Got a cold coming, I think,' she fabricated quickly. 'I only came—'

'Mary, bring some coffee, would you?' she interrupted. 'And—'

'No, truly, I can't stop, but I thought I would like to get on with the portrait at home this weekend.' Glancing at the clock, Sarah saw that it was gone nine-thirty and hurried across to the easel. 'I'll just take it all as it is…' She grabbed her paint box, and, carefully so as not to damage the painting, she hoisted the easel under her arm. She gave another bright smile. 'Right, well, I'm off. Sorry to have disturbed you. Goodbye.' Knowing she was going to cry, she hurried out, shoved everything into the back of the car, and drove away.

Taking small, snatched breaths, she held her eyes wide to stop the tears as she drove back to the house. She parked quietly outside the garage, then ran in to collect her suitcase, unpinned the painting from the easel and rolled it up carefully, before she began hurrying towards the village.

'Something wrong?' Duncan asked quietly.

'What? No, sorry,' Jed apologised, 'just…' Just a feeling that something wasn't quite right. A small frown dug into his face as he stared out at the passing scenery. She'd been crying, of course, but that didn't mean… Perhaps she'd finally come to the realisation that it wasn't going to work, that pretending was no way to live your life. She'd looked so heartbroken…

He'd thought the pain in his head and leg were bad enough, but compared to emotional pain they were nothing. He couldn't leave her alone like that, could he? Barely paying attention to Duncan, his mind distracted, he said suddenly, 'I need to go back. Duncan, I'm sorry, but I need to go back.' Feeling a sudden sense of urgency, an urgency that had always served him well in the past, a sense of—danger, that had more than once saved his life, he turned to his friend. 'Would you take me back?'

'Back?'

'Yes, to the house. I can't explain, I just…'

'Need to go back,' Duncan finished for him with wry resignation. 'OK. But if this car turns out to be the bargain I think it is, and I lose out, I'll…' Without finishing, he pulled into the side of the road, checked the traffic, and did a quick U-turn.

'Writers,' he grumbled amiably. 'I suppose you've just thought of a wonderful plot…'

'Yes,' he agreed, because to say anything else, explain his fears, would sound stupid. Not that he particularly minded looking stupid, and if his gut feeling turned out to be false then there was no harm done. But if it wasn't false… 'Thanks,' he said gratefully. 'I owe you one.'

When Duncan dropped him off, he stared at the car in relief, and then noticed the easel in

the back. Frowning, he hurried indoors.
'Sarah?' he called. Nothing.

Checking each room with more and more
urgency, he finally opened her bedroom door
and stared inside. A sick feeling in his stomach, he saw the note propped on her dressing
table and quickly snatched it up.

Opening it with hands that shook, he began
to read it, and then had to take a deep breath
and start again. Oh, Sarah. Galvanised into action he hurried out. Where had she gone? *How*
had she gone? Mrs McKenzie might know;
Sarah had obviously been there. Stumbling
down the stairs, he nearly knocked Mrs
Reeves flying as she came in through the front
door. He grabbed her, steadied her. 'Sorry,' he
apologised quickly. 'Can't stop.'

'No,' she agreed. 'I did wonder why she
was going on the bus.'

Halfway out the front door, he halted,
turned back. 'What?'

'Sarah,' she explained impatiently.

Grabbing her arm, he demanded urgently,
'What about Sarah?'

'The bus!' she exclaimed. 'I said I wondered why she was getting on the bus!'

'What bus?'

'The one from the village!'

'To Glasgow?'

'Well, of course to Glasgow! What other bus do we have?'

'None. Thank you!' he said fervently, kissed her and hurried out.

Staring after him in shock, she pursed her lips, shook her head and walked towards the kitchen. They must have had a row, she supposed. Well, he had plenty of time to catch her. That bus took for ever.

Climbing into the car, he glanced at his watch, switched on the ignition—and then switched it off. The bus didn't get into Glasgow until midday, and even when he found her, whatever happened, he was certainly not going to drive all the way back here again. Getting out of the car, he hurried back into the house. Ignoring the pain in his leg; ignoring Mrs Reeves' call of enquiry from the kitchen, he went up to his room, shoved a few changes of clothing into a holdall and limped back downstairs. His leg protesting every step of the way, he went to find Mrs Reeves to explain that he would be away for a few days. Five minutes later, he was back in the car and heading towards Glasgow. He might be wrong, he kept telling himself. Her letter hadn't exactly made a great deal of sense, but he needed to know. For certain.

There was nowhere to park at the bus station and he wasted precious minutes trying to find somewhere before hurrying back to wait for the bus, and then tried to laugh at himself because he still had over half an hour to wait.

Too impatient to keep still, he strode up and down in the freezing wind until his leg was screaming in agony. Ignoring it, shutting his mind to it, he finally saw the bus trundling its slow way into the stop. Stepping back into the shelter so that she wouldn't immediately see him, he scanned the people descending. He couldn't see her at first, and felt a momentary panic that Mrs Reeves had been wrong, or that Sarah had got off at another stop. Idiot, he scolded himself, he should have caught up with the bus, followed it... But then he saw her. She looked little and sad, her ridiculous hat pulled down over her ears, and he felt his heart lurch. Unable to wait any longer, he stepped forward.

As though she knew, or could feel him watching her, she halted on the steps, looked up, and froze. Her eyes seemed too big, too brown, he thought, feeling he could weep for her obvious sorrow.

Someone pushed her impatiently from behind, and she stumbled. Hurrying forward, he
caught her, took her case from her hand, and,
oblivious to the people milling round them trying to get past, his expression almost austere,
he demanded abruptly, 'Do you love me,
Sarah?'

Feeling helpless and tired, so achingly tired,
she closed her eyes for a moment.

'Do you? Because this has to stop now,' he
added with a decisiveness she hadn't heard
from him for a long, long while. 'I've been
behaving as I was never meant to behave, be-
lieving things that maybe weren't true, making
assumptions, and it has to be resolved, here,
now. So do you?'

Searching his face, his eyes, knowing she
had no more strength, no more fight left in her,
she whispered quietly, 'I was giving you your
freedom.'

'And if I don't want it?' he asked urgently.

'But you do,' she began helplessly. 'I've stifled you, hurt you...'

'Answer me,' he insisted. 'If I don't?'

'And you said yourself you would never
have married me if I hadn't been pregnant.'

'For your sake, not mine. Now tell me.'

'My sake?' she asked in bewilderment.

'Yes. Do you *love* me?' he persisted urgently.

Wanting to lie, needing to lie, she just stared at him until he dropped the case and gave her a little shake.

'Yes,' she whispered, 'but...'

'Yes, what?'

'Yes, I love you. More than life itself,' she added almost too softly for him to hear. 'So, you see, that's why—'

Her words were cut off by his mouth. His face still set, almost harsh, he kissed her. Properly. Hungrily. Dragged her into his arms and kissed her as though he were never going to stop.

Too surprised for a moment to react, she just stood there, and then, with a little cry, she clutched him tight and kissed him back.

In the busy station, amongst all the crowds and the bustle, they kissed with an urgency, a desperation, that made the passing strangers smile. It went on for a very long time. An eternity. With her neck cricked, her body aching, she eventually dragged her mouth away, burrowing her face into his neck and burst into tears.

His cheek against her hair, and his eyes closed, he held her against him with enough force to crush her ribs, soothing her with words he couldn't afterwards recall. And then, when her crying subsided, having turned into shaky gasps, he muttered huskily, 'Let's get out of here.' Thrusting her away, he picked up her case, grabbed her arm and led her towards the exit.

'Not back to the house…' she began breathlessly.

'No. We'll find a hotel.'

She was forced to take little skipping steps to keep up with him, until they reached the car. Then she gasped when he dropped the case and dragged her back into his arms, kissing her again with a ruthless urgency that left her shaking.

They were staring at each other, just staring; she reached up a trembling hand to touch his mouth. 'I thought you no longer wanted me.'

'And I thought the same.'

'What?'

'Only I couldn't bear it.' Crushing her against him, mouth against her hair, he repeated softly, 'I couldn't bear it. I always knew that one day I would hurt you, I just never suspected how much.'

'No,' she denied against his chest.

'Yes. But why on earth would you think I wanted *my* freedom?'

'Because I was just getting in your way, stifling you...'

'Don't be a fool.'

'I'm not!' Finding it hard to talk muffled against his chest, she forced her head free and looked up at him. 'Everyone was surprised you were married,' she began earnestly, her eyes wide. 'They said you were a loner, could never imagine you with babies—'

'Sarah!' he interrupted. 'You're my reason for *living*!' As though he couldn't bear to say more, not yet, he opened the door, ushered her quickly inside, tossed her case into the back, climbed behind the wheel and drove quickly away.

'But...'

'Not now, not when I'm driving.' He sounded terse, distracted as he reached for her hand and squeezed it painfully.

'Really?' she asked again as she continued to stare at him. 'You really want me?'

'Dear God, yes.'

Pulling into the forecourt of the first hotel they came to, a rather large and imposing Victorian structure, he led her inside to an oasis of peace and quiet. Rather old-fashioned, but comforting. Jed registered, collected the key, handed over the car keys for someone to collect the luggage, and she watched him. Tall, slender, and with an authority that seemed natural. Some people were deferred to automatically, simply because of who they were. Jed was one of them. And he'd kissed her. Properly. She was his reason for living?

Dazed, almost disbelieving, she allowed Jed to lead her into the lift in the wake of a red-capped bellboy. He didn't look at her, or make eye contact, but his hand crushed hers as they rode to the third floor in silence. And he was tense. So very tense. Following the boy along the corridor, they halted at a door at the end. It was thrown open to reveal a small sitting room. Jed tipped the boy and instructed quietly, 'You don't need to hurry with the luggage.'

He didn't so much as smirk. 'Very well, sir. Enjoy your stay.'

'We intend to.' Closing the door on him, he turned back to Sarah. 'Don't we?' he asked thickly.

'Yes. I don't understand...' she began.

'Understanding can wait. Can't it? Come here.'

More than happy to obey, she tossed off her

coat and walked into his arms. 'Don't let me go.'

'I don't intend to.'

Undoing his coat, she burrowed inside, slid her arms round him and rested her head against his chest. Breathing in the scent of him, the warmth, she whispered, 'It's been so hard.'

'For both of us. I never considered myself a fool, until now.'

'I thought you wanted Deanna…'

'Never. You really think I wanted a wife whose behaviour is dictated by boredom?'

'No, but—but she's so beautiful.'

'So are you.'

'No…'

'Yes.'

Lifting her head, needing to see him, she released one hand and touched it to his face. 'It would have been easier if she'd been hateful. But she wasn't. I even quite liked her.'

'So do I, but not as my wife. I think the bedroom's that way.'

Her smile was shaky. 'Do you have any idea how often I've longed to hear you say those words?'

'Do you know how often I've longed to say them?' he countered. Scooping her up, he carried her through the far door and lay her on the wide bed. Removing his coat, his shoes, and then her own, he lay beside her and pulled her into his arms. 'Explanations can wait. Can't they?'

'Yes.'

Between kisses and hugs, touching, shivering with need and urgency, she helped him remove his clothes, as he helped her.

'Make love to me.'

'I intend to.'

The room was warm, the bed soft, and when the first, urgent need was over they lay entwined, kissing, touching, loving. Soft words, murmured exchanges, and as the room darkened around them they snuggled closer and closed their eyes. They didn't sleep for long, just an hour or so, and when they woke they made love again.

'Shower? Bath?' he asked softly as he traced his long fingers across her face.

'Bath. I never knew if you loved me, Jed.'

'How could you not know? I adore the very ground you walk on.'

'Do you?'

'Yes.'

'But after the accident...'

'The reason for our marriage was gone—and I thought you wanted out.'

'No…'

'I always knew how reluctant you were to marry me…'

'For *your* sake!' she protested. 'Not mine! I felt I was *trapping* you.'

'And I thought the same,' he said with a wry smile. 'And who would think that two such articulate people could behave so daftly? I never knew if you wanted to hear the words I always wanted to say. I'd never been in love before, not like that. I had no idea it would be so complicated. And then, after the accident, I was afraid to ask…'

'So was I.'

'And every time you said you wanted to talk about it, I shied away in fear. I was afraid of losing you, and then afraid to beg you stay.'

Touching his face, needing the feel of him against her, still hardly daring to believe it was all right, she whispered, 'I love you.'

'As I love you. More than you will ever know, I think. Come on.' With a gentle kiss, he rolled to his feet and held out his hand. Putting her own into it, she walked with him into the rather opulent bathroom. Screwing her hair up on top of her head and securing it with one of the clips provided by the hotel, she bent to put the plug in and his long fingers touched her spine, her hips, began stroking erotically down her body. She reached to turn on the taps, closing her eyes in ecstasy as he continued to massage her, touch her. Arms hanging down into the water, she felt his arousal against her and shuddered. She'd waited so long for this, had feared it would never happen again, and her breath hitched in her throat as emotion threatened to overwhelm her.

He climbed into the bath first, emptied in several sachets without looking to see what they were, and then helped her in to join him.

'I think one of them was shampoo.' She laughed as froth bubbled up to encompass them.

'Don't care. Do you?'

'No,' she agreed as she lay on top of him. Nose to nose, they shared a grin, and then the grin faded as they both came to the realisation of how important this was. How much it was needed.

'How did you know where I was?' she asked softly as she began to rub her hands over his chest, his arms, shoulders.

'Mrs Reeves saw you getting on the bus.'

'But you were with Duncan…'

'I came back. Oh, Sarah!' he exclaimed softly. 'Not to love you, not to hold you—I don't think I ever believed that such a bright, happy girl could care for me. I felt so guilty after the accident...'

'Shh.'

With a deep, ragged breath, he held her close. 'No one ever explained how hard it would be to watch you despair, lose weight, cry. And I didn't think this day would ever come,' he said raggedly as he turned her to the side and rolled to face her.

'Neither did I.'

Slick as seals, stretching luxuriantly in the warm water, they soaped each other, taking their time, taking pleasure, and when the water cooled they climbed out, shrugged into the robes the hotel had provided and went back to lay on the bed. Opening her robe, he began to kiss her. Her breasts, ribs, waist. He savoured the warmth of her, the taste, smiled when she squirmed beneath his touch.

'Do you want to eat up here, or in the restaurant?' he asked absently as he continued his exploration.

'Here. I don't want to share you with anyone. Not yet.'

'Good.' Moving to her mouth, he kissed her

thoroughly before hitching himself up and picking up the bedside phone to dial room service.

Sarah watched him. His hair was wet, as was hers, and a little runnel of water was sliding down over the scar on his forehead. Putting out a finger, she gently trapped it. Being able to hold him again, touch him, was a joy she didn't think she would ever get tired of. Trailing her finger down his cheek, to his jaw, and then into the neck of his robe, she slid her hand inside, and felt his muscles contract. His voice changed as he spoke into the phone, and she grinned, and then as quickly sobered as she wondered what would have happened if he hadn't stopped her at the bus station.

'What's wrong?' he asked gently as he replaced the receiver and turned towards her.

'I was just wondering what would have happened if you hadn't stopped me. If Mrs Reeves hadn't seen me. I had it all planned, you see. I was going to disappear. After meeting Deanna, seeing you with her, I thought it would be kinder to leave. I knew you wouldn't let me go if you thought I loved you, but I couldn't bear the thought that you would stay with me out of duty, or responsibility.'

Searching his face, his eyes, she added softly, 'I felt so guilty and stupid and frightened. All used up, especially after…'

'You saw me kissing her.'

'Yes.'

'A kiss of friendship, nothing more. She'd been…'

'Upset?'

'Yes. I think she thought we would both stay the same. Never marrying, always there for each other, and maybe it would have been like that if I hadn't met you. Fallen in love. But when I knew you'd seen us, it seemed— easier not to explain because I thought you no longer loved me. If you ever had. Or perhaps I was hoping for a sign of jealousy. And then I would have known how you felt.'

'And I thought you married me because of your own circumstances, out of duty. Because of having no father.'

'No. You have no idea, do you?'

'About what?'

'How I feel about you.'

'I do *now*,' she admitted. 'But not before, no. I always knew, or thought I knew, that I loved you more than you loved me. Why did you say it was for my sake you wouldn't have married me if I hadn't been pregnant?'

'Because I never imagined I would marry. Besides I thought myself too old for you,' he explained as he touched gentle fingers to her neck.

'It's only eight years.'

'I didn't mean in age, but in spirit, soul. I'd seen too much, done too much, and you were such an innocent.'

'Not that innocent,' she protested. 'I went halfway round the world by myself!'

He gave a small smile. 'So you did. But people look after you, don't they? Take you under their wing. I'm not saying you can't look after yourself, only that you bring out protective instincts in people. Including me. Writing is a pretty solitary occupation,' he explained. 'You would be on your own a lot...'

'I'm not a child, Jed. Although,' she added honestly, 'I think I've behaved pretty childishly in the past. But now, now I feel very old. All grown up,' she added seriously. 'After everything that happened...'

'Yes. I think we've both changed. But when you told me you were pregnant, I was so pleased.'

'Pleased?' she asked in surprise.

'Yes, because then there wasn't a choice. I had to marry you. And then it was what I

wanted above all things. The guilt I'd felt that
I might be robbing you of your youth if I'd
asked you to marry me before was swept
away. To have a family of my own, something
I thought I would never have…' Breaking off,
he rolled to his feet and went to stand at the
window as though the emotion of it all was
momentarily too much.

'When the doctor came,' he continued after
a moment, 'after I'd been moved from intensive care, and he told me that you'd lost the
baby, I wanted to cry. They wouldn't let me
see you, said you were resting.'

'Worried sick,' she corrected, 'and I had
been trying to get in to see you too.'

He gave a small bleak smile that she didn't
see. 'I thought you blamed me, as I blamed
myself. And when we got home, that night you
wanted to make love to me, there was such a
desperation about you, I thought it was out of
pity: that you were trying to *pretend* that you
still loved me, had forgiven me…'

'No,' she denied in distress.

'And so I tried to think of you, not of myself. I sat in that study day after day, night
after night, doing nothing. Worried sick about
you, feeling helpless and desperate. I'd wanted

that baby so much. Wanted you. That was when I began to think I should let you go.'

Climbing from the bed, feeling almost bereft without the feel of him against her, she walked to slide her arms round him, rest her head against his back. 'And I thought I'd trapped you.'

'No, never that.' Holding her hands warmly against his stomach, he murmured softly, 'You made me feel young again. Your innocent pleasure in things delighted me, but I fought against wanting you for a very long time. Until you came into my room. The day we became lovers will stay with me for ever.'

'But you…'

'Never gave all of myself? No, because I thought you would come to your senses. I couldn't for the life of me imagine why you would want me. So young, so pretty, all the world before you, I thought you would soon get tired of a cynical old devil like me.'

'Jed,' she protested on a half-laugh. 'You never gave the impression of lacking in *confidence*!'

'I wasn't.' He smiled. 'I just thought that one day you would find someone else. Someone younger.'

'And I always thought you would want

someone more sophisticated, beautiful, elegant.'

'No, and I don't think you will ever understand how much you mean to me. I never learned how to say it, how to tell you. I don't share things, do I? I never learned how.'

'Oh, Jed,' she whispered sadly.

'But after the accident,' he continued, 'when I couldn't do anything for you, couldn't make it better, when I had to stand by and watch you struggle with your pain and loss because I thought your smiles and your kisses were to try and spare my feelings... Dear God, Sarah,' he exclaimed fervently, 'I don't ever want to go through something like that again!' Turning in the circle of her arms, he held her shoulders, stared down into her face. 'Don't you know you're my reason for being? That one look from those big brown eyes can melt my heart?'

'No,' she whispered. 'I thought you quite liked me, but...'

He gave a small smile. 'It's a whole lot more than "quite like."'

'Perhaps if I'd never heard about Deanna, seen her—she made me feel very inadequate,' she confessed. 'But then, I imagine she makes

most women feel inadequate. She looks so—
exciting.'

'And you don't think you are?'

She pulled a face. 'Well, no.'

'Remembering what happened here, in that
bed, and in the bath, you really don't think you
excite me?'

She crossed her eyes at him and he laughed,
hugged her warmly against him.

'Your humour, your energetic enjoyment of
everything, delights me. I used to sit up in my
room in the eaves in Bavaria and listen to you
chatting to tourists as you painted them. Listen
to you laugh. So at ease with people as though
you expect everyone to be your friend. And
they are. That was the thing I found so ex-
traordinary. They all were.'

His mobile suddenly beeped, and, pulling
her with him, he limped across to answer it.

'Hello?'

'Jed? It's Fiona. Jed, what's going on? Mrs
Reeves said Sarah left on the bus and—'

'She did. A small misunderstanding, that's
all.'

'Is she all right? Only Mum said she seemed
upset…'

Glancing down at his wife as she stood in

the circle of his arms, he reassured her, 'Sarah's fine.'

'Can I speak to her?'

'No.'

'Why?'

'Because she's busy. I'll call you later.' He broke the connection and put the phone back on the bedside table. 'Aren't you?' he asked her softly.

'Very.' Sliding her arms round him, she pressed a warm kiss to his nipple, extended her tongue, just as there was a soft tap on the outer door.

He gave a small *moue* of disappointment and kissed her nose. 'Our dinner, I expect. Are you dressing?'

'No,' she denied, her eyes alight with love.

'Good.' Retying his belt, he went to open the door.

Jed called her, and she walked slowly to join him. Their luggage sat on the floor, the easel balanced on top. 'You're expecting me to *work*?'

'No—' he laughed '—it was in the car. I'd have liked to have seen the painting. You finished it?'

'No, it's in my case, hopefully not damaged.'

'We'll look later, but, for now, come and eat your dinner before it gets cold.'

Glancing at the trolley that sat by the table, she obediently took her place.

Jed served her, touched her each time he passed, and when they'd finished eating she picked up her glass and silently toasted him. 'You're too far away,' she murmured, and then smiled as he shuffled his chair round next to her.

'Better?'

'Much.'

They kissed, a long, lingering exchange that tasted of wine, and then she had a sudden thought, felt her stomach contract. 'Jed?'

'Mmm?'

'We didn't take any precautions.'

He stared at her, searched her face. 'No,' he agreed. 'Is it too soon? Will it—?'

'No,' she interrupted. 'I'm a bit scared, but…'

Taking her hand in his, he clasped her fingers tight. 'What will be, will be?'

'Yes.'

'We love each other. It will be all right. We see the doctor next week…'

'Yes,' she agreed.

'He'll advise us. We'll stay here until then,

and then we'll head south, look for a house near to your grandmother if that's what you'd like. Find a base for ourselves.'

'Is it what you want?'

'Yes. I want a proper home, with a garden. A family. I'll put the house here up for sale, I think. Time to move on.'

'And perhaps next summer we could go back to Bavaria, see our friends there. Visit that lovely lake at the foot of the Zugspitze.'

'The Eibsee, yes. Back to bed?'

She smiled at him. 'Back to bed,' she agreed.

'Is it bad?'

'Yes, no,' Sarah gasped as the pain hooked granite fingers into her back.

'Well, please don't have it until we get to the hospital,' Jed pleaded as he helped her in and hastily fitted her seat belt over her bump. 'I don't think I'll be very good as a midwife.'

'I'm certain of it,' she agreed as she took deep, panting breaths.

'Oh, God.' Closing her door, he climbed behind the wheel, and, although she knew he wanted to drive like a bat out of hell, he managed to restrain himself.

There was plenty of time. Probably. Hopefully. It was only a ten-minute drive to the hospital, but she suspected to Jed it felt like hours. Dark lanes, ghostly hedges, and a full moon to light their way. Staring fixedly at the dashboard clock, she timed her contractions, began to pant again as she'd been taught.

His quick glances at her were unnerving and she instructed him to watch the road.

'Yes,' he agreed. 'Sarah, I wasn't going to be like this. I really wasn't. I'm shaking so much…'

'It's all right,' she soothed. 'Just calm down. Not long now, I can see the lights ahead.'

She didn't know who was more relieved, herself or Jed, when the hospital came in sight.

Pulling up outside the maternity unit, he began to help her out, then stopped. 'No, wait,' he urged, 'I'll get you a wheelchair.'

'I'm all right.'

'No, you aren't.' He dashed off, leaving Sarah half in, half out of the car, and she took another deep breath, prayed he would hurry up as the cold wind explored her ankles.

Moments later he was back with a porter pushing a wheelchair.

'You can't leave that car here…' he began.

'Watch me,' Jed muttered as he helped Sarah out and into the wheelchair. The man laughed. He'd seen it all before.

'Just park it over there, there's a good lad,' he instructed. 'You're blocking the entrance.'

With a curse, Jed instructed forcefully, 'Don't go without me.' Climbing back into the car, he drove off a short distance, stopped, switched off and slammed the door.

'I'd lock it if I were you.'

With another curse, he walked back, locked the car and strode back to his wife. 'You should have taken her inside! She'll freeze out here!'

'You told me to wait.'

'I didn't mean *here*! Come on, let's go. All right?' he asked Sarah.

'Fine.' Poor Jed.

His patience was tested to the limit as she was booked in, taken to a side room, interviewed, instructed, examined whilst Jed prowled around like the expectant father he was.

'Shouldn't we have a doctor?' he demanded.

'No,' the nurse denied amiably. 'Go and sit down. You've ages yet.'

Staring at her in horror, he exclaimed, 'What?'

'Ages,' she repeated. 'Go and get a cup of tea.'

Thrusting his hands through his hair, he took a deep breath. 'How long?'

'Hours.'

'Hours?'

'Mmm-hmm. OK, Mrs Dane, get undressed

and into bed. I'll come and check on you in a bit.'

'You're going to *leave* her?'

She laughed. 'Yes. I'm going to leave her. Now be a good boy and calm down.'

As she walked out, he grasped the bed rail with both hands and slumped. 'We won't have any more,' he said fervently.

'You haven't had this one yet,' Sarah pointed out.

Raising his eyes, he stared at her and gave a sheepish smile. 'Fat lot of good I am.'

'But I need you here,' she said simply. 'You don't have to do anything, just be here for me.'

'Of course I'll be here for you. You don't think I'm going to *leave*, do you?' Walking round the bed, he sat down beside her and took her hand in his. 'I rang Duncan a few days ago,' he confessed. 'Asked him how it would be. "Don't ask," he said. He sounded as though he shuddered.'

Stifling a smile, she stared at this husband of hers, and so much love welled up inside her that her eyes pricked with tears. His hair was uncombed, his chin beginning to get stubbley, and she loved him to bits. She'd been so nervous when she'd first known she was pregnant, but there had been no terrible hormone changes this time, no drastic mood swings; the pregnancy had been easy and uncomplicated. She'd had cravings for peanut butter, which she normally hated, but that was about all. And cramp, of course, and heartburn. And soon, very soon now, she was going to be a mummy. She could barely imagine it, barely comprehend how their lives were going to change. A year almost to the day since they had booked into that hotel outside Glasgow. A year of happiness, of finding their house, going to Bavaria to visit their friends, of having Fiona and Duncan to stay with their new baby. A little boy. James.

She'd finished the painting of Mrs McKenzie and sent it to her. She'd had a very nice note back.

Gripping Jed's hands tight as another pain cramped her insides, she then sighed, and leaned back.

'All right?' he asked gently.

'Yes.'

'I didn't think it would take this long.'

'No,' she agreed. She'd left it as late as she could before coming in, left it as late as she'd dared and now she just wanted it over.

'Come on, let's get you undressed and into bed.'

She was examined periodically, the dilation checked, and all she wanted to do was go to sleep, but every time she drifted off, her hands still in Jed's, the pain would wake her.

Three hours later, too tired to feel excited, she was wheeled along to the delivery room. Jed stayed with her, held her, pushed with her, and two hours after *that*, she finally gave birth to a little girl.

Tired, sleepy, so *very* glad it was over, slightly ashamed of the fuss she thought she'd made, and so *thankful* there was no more pushing to be done, she stared at the little bundle in her arms and a lone tear trickled down to plop onto the baby's cheek. Glancing at Jed as he stared at his daughter, she swallowed hard when he turned away and pressed thumb and forefinger against his eyes for a moment. She saw the deep breath he took, saw how his hands shook, and reached out to touch his arm.

'All over,' she said softly.

'Yes,' he agreed thickly. 'Sarah, I want to weep. I love you so much.' Extending his hand, he touched one trembling finger to the baby's fist.

'Do you want to hold her for a minute before they take her away to be cleaned up?'

'No. Yes.'

The midwife, who had been watching the exchange, grinned and gently took the baby from Sarah and handed her to Jed.

Holding his daughter in his arms, more emotional than he would ever have believed possible, he stared down at the crumpled face. 'She isn't crying.'

'No.' The midwife smiled. 'Make the most of it. It won't last. Go on, go and get a cup of tea or something,' she added as she took the baby from him and handed her to her assistant. 'We have to clean your wife up, put in a couple of stitches. Come back in an hour.'

Looking dazed and exhausted himself, he bent to kiss Sarah, a long, lingering kiss full of love and relief, and then walked out.

Pushing out into the fresh air, surprised to find that it was daylight, he dragged in deep lungfuls of crisp, cold air. A daughter. And he didn't have any family to ring. And it hurt, he found. Grow up, Jed, he scolded himself. You're thirty-five. Taking a few more deep breaths, he walked to his car and sagged thankfully into the seat. He didn't think he had ever been so exhausted in his entire life.

Taking his mobile from the glove compart-
ment, he checked his watch, and, seeing that
it was just gone eight, he rang Sarah's grandmother to tell her she had a great-
granddaughter. And that was when it sank in.
He was a father. A proud and happy, ecstatic
father. Daddy. He wanted to weep again. And
he'd forgotten to ask how much she weighed.
Forgotten to ask if they were still to call her
Athena after Sarah's mother. Sarah had remembered to ask if the baby was all right, he
remembered that. And she was. Perfect in
every respect. He could phone Fiona. And
Gita in Bavaria, but he had to get flowers,
shower and shave, get a teddy bear.

A wide smile on his face, a bit shaky, a bit
wobbly, he thanked God for miracles and
drove home.

An hour and a half later, he walked back
into the hospital, showered, shaved, tired, but
on a high with two dozen red roses and a teddy
with a pink bow in his arms. Very eager to
see his Sarah and his new daughter.

A heavily pregnant woman gave him an interested glance, and he laughed in sheer relief
that it was all over. He wasn't sure he could
go through all that again. One daughter would
suit him just fine.

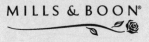

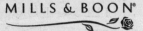

MILLS & BOON®

Presents...™

THE UNEXPECTED HUSBAND by *Lindsay Armstrong*

Lydia was thrilled by her assignment on an Australian cattle station—until she came face to face with tough, sexy Joe Jordan on her first day. Joe made it clear that he wanted to marry her! But did he just want a convenient wife?

A SUSPICIOUS PROPOSAL by *Helen Brooks*

Millionaire business man Xavier Grey seemed intent on pursuing Essie. And he was used to getting what he wanted! But when he proposed, was it an affair or marriage he had in mind...and could Essie trust him?

THE SURROGATE MOTHER by *Lilian Darcy*

After her cousin's death, surrogate mother Julie was suddenly the *only* mother for the baby she was carrying. But, when the baby's father, Tom Callahan, insisted on marriage, Julie feared he'd never see her as anything but a surrogate—wife, mother or lover...

CONTRACT BRIDEGROOM by *Sandra Field*

Celia wanted to grant her dying father's wish to see her 'happily married', so she was paying Jethro Lathem to be her temporary husband. Then she discovered Jethro was a multimillionaire! Why on earth had he agreed to marry her? Moreover, their 'no sex' agreement was proving to be a nightmare—for both of them!

Available from 7th July 2000

0006/01a

MILLS & BOON®

Presents...™

THE COZAKIS BRIDE by *Lynne Graham*

Olivia had no choice: her mother urgently needed expensive medical treatment, so she'd have to beg Nik Cozakis to marry her. Nik agreed, but only if Olivia bore him a son…

ROMANO'S REVENGE by *Sandra Marton*

When Joe's new cook turned out to be blonde, beautiful—and useless in the kitchen—he knew it was the work of his matchmaking grandmother. So he decided to add posing as his fiancée to Lucinda's list of duties. Lucinda could cope with a pretend engagement—but she drew the line at sharing Joe's bed!

THE MILLIONAIRE'S VIRGIN by *Anne Mather*

Nikolas has obviously not forgiven Paige for walking out on him four years ago. So why has he offered her a job on his Greek island for the summer? And what exactly will he be expecting from her?

THE PLAYBOY'S PROPOSITION by *Miranda Lee*

Tyler Garrison was impossibly handsome, and heir to a fortune. So Michele was touched by his plan to escort her to her ex-boyfriend's wedding as her pretend lover. But she was shocked when he proposed they become lovers for real—what was his motive?

Available from 7th July 2000

Emma Darcy brings you...

Kings of the **OUTBACK**

Meet the Kings, three brothers with three very different lifestyles, all living in the outback of Australia. Join the Kings of the Outback in their search for soulmates.

The Playboy King's Wife

4th August

The Pleasure King's Bride

3rd November

FREE
4 BOOKS
AND A SURPRISE GIFT!

We would like to take this opportunity to thank you for reading this Mills & Boon® book by offering you the chance to take FOUR more specially selected titles from the Presents...™ series absolutely FREE! We're also making this offer to introduce you to the benefits of the Reader Service™ —

- ★ FREE home delivery
- ★ FREE monthly Newsletter
- ★ FREE gifts and competitions
- ★ Exclusive Reader Service discounts
- ★ Books available before they're in the shops

Accepting these FREE books and gift places you under no obligation to buy; you may cancel at any time, even after receiving your free shipment. Simply complete your details below and return the entire page to the address below. *You don't even need a stamp!*

YES! Please send me 4 free Presents...™ books and a surprise gift. I understand that unless you hear from me, I will receive 6 superb new titles every month for just £2.40 each, postage and packing free. I am under no obligation to purchase any books and may cancel my subscription at any time. The free books and gift will be mine to keep in any case. P0EC

Ms/Mrs/Miss/Mr ....Initials ....
                                                                                    BLOCK CAPITALS PLEASE
Surname ....

Address ....

....

....Postcode ....

Send this whole page to:
UK: FREEPOST CN81, Croydon, CR9 3WZ
EIRE: PO Box 4546, Kilcock, County Kildare (stamp required)

Offer valid in UK and Eire only and not available to current Reader Service subscribers to this series. We reserve the right to refuse an application and applicants must be aged 18 years or over. Only one application per household. Terms and prices subject to change without notice. Offer expires 31st December 2000. As a result of this application, you may receive further offers from Harlequin Mills & Boon Limited and other carefully selected companies. If you would prefer not to share in this opportunity please write to The Data Manager at the address above.

Mills & Boon® is a registered trademark owned by Harlequin Mills & Boon Limited.
Presents...™ is being used as a trademark.